THE
FAMILIAR
DARK

ALSO BY AMY ENGEL

The Roanoke Girls
The Book of Ivy
The Revolution of Ivy

THE
FAMILIAR
DARK

A Novel

AMY ENGEL

DUTTON

DUTTON

An imprint of Penguin Random House LLC
penguinrandomhouse.com

LIBRARY OF CONGRESS CATALOGING-IN-PUBLICATION DATA
Names: Engel, Amy, author.
Title: The familiar dark: a novel / Amy Engel.
Description: [New York] : Dutton, [2020] |
Identifiers: LCCN 2019025265 (print) | LCCN 2019025266 (ebook) |
ISBN 9781524745950 (hardcover) | ISBN 9781524746018 (ebook)
Subjects: LCSH: Grief—Fiction. | Murder—Investigation—Fiction. | GSAFD:
Mystery fiction.
Classification: LCC PS3605.N4354 F36 2020 (print) | LCC PS3605.N4354
(ebook) | DDC 813/.6—dc23
LC record available at https://lccn.loc.gov/2019025265
LC ebook record available at https://lccn.loc.gov/2019025266

International edition ISBN: 9781524746391

Printed in the United States of America
1   3   5   7   9   10   8   6   4   2

BOOK DESIGN BY TIFFANY ESTREICHER

For Graham and Quinn, my brightest lights

We grow accustomed to the Dark—
When Light is put away—

—Emily Dickinson

THE
FAMILIAR
DARK

THE END

They died during a freak April snowstorm, blood pooling on a patchy bed of white. Afterward, some people said the killer must have kept an eye on the gathering gray clouds. Taken the weather as a cue to strike and picked the moment when everyone else was huddled indoors, shivering in their optimistic shirtsleeves and muttering about global warming. Armchair detectives trying to make sense of something that would never be anything but senseless. They were wrong, of course. It had nothing to do with the weather. The girls could have told them that, if the girls had been capable of speaking.

Izzy died first, dark brown hair tangled over her face and one eye peeking out between the strands. A slow blink, gaze trained on Junie's face. Another blink, focus fading. Junie waited for a third blink that never came, watched blood unspool in the space between them. She tried to reach for Izzy, meaning to shake her back into the world, but couldn't make her own hand move. It felt weighted down even though she couldn't remember being tied up. Couldn't remember anything, really. Why she was here or what was happening. Only a dim, distant terror that pulsed along with her fading heartbeat. She pushed a sound out of her ruined throat, a name, a plea, a prayer. But it never made it past her lips. A bubble of blood popped and spilled over. The snow pressed cold against her cheek.

"Shhh . . ." a voice said. "It'll be over soon. Shhh . . ." A hand on her head, stroking her hair.

She tilted her eyes upward, the only part of her body she could seem to move. Saw the edge of the swing set, a branch coated in white, the flat, iron gray sky. Last time she'd been here was with her mother. They'd had ice cream that melted down their hands faster than they could eat it. Hot, sweaty dusk and fireflies. Swinging side by side and Junie's mother jumping off her swing at its highest arc, blond hair whipping out behind her, throaty laugh cutting through the air. Telling Junie the secret was not to think about it. Close your eyes and fly.

Mama. The longing tore through her like a barbed hook, her body bucking once against the ground, her hand spasming into a fist. *I want my mama.* She smelled her mother's perfume, a spring garden doled out a single drop at a time to make the bottle last. She heard her mother's voice, whispering comfort into the shell of her ear. She tasted salt, tears on her lips and blood in her mouth. She knew this was the end, and couldn't believe it was coming so close to the beginning. A sigh shuddered out of her. *Watch me, Mama. I can do it.* She closed her eyes and soared.

ONE

I'd had one eye on the clock all day. Had taken heaps of shit for it, too. Every time I'd leaned over the counter to pick up an order, Thomas had swatted at my hand with his grease-spattered spatula. "You got somewhere else you need to be?" he asked, tsking under his breath. "Yeah, somewhere better than this crap hole," I shot back, laughing when he went for me with the spatula again. That was about the only good thing I could find in having worked in this dump for more than a decade: I didn't have to mind my manners anymore.

"It's almost five o'clock," I called out, after watching the minute hand creep around the clock one final time.

"What's your hurry today, anyway?" Louise asked, retying her apron around her thick waist. "You're like a cat in a room full of rocking chairs. Keep it up and you're gonna give Thomas a heart attack. You know he hates it when we're distracted."

I threw a glance back through the pickup window, winked at Thomas, who couldn't quite manage to keep his scowl in place. "I don't know," I admitted. "Antsy, I guess." Maybe it was the strange, unexpected weather. Yesterday had been a budding, whispery green, the air scented with wildflowers. Today snow had splattered against the diner's plate glass windows, tiny swirls sneaking inside every time someone opened the door. But now the sun was starting to peek out from behind the cloud cover, just in time for it to set. Already rivulets of melting snow were forming on the edges of the parking lot. By morning it would be spring again. But that was Missouri for you. Like the old-timers always said, if you don't like the weather, wait five minutes.

"Coulda been those sirens," Thomas offered. "Damn things about drove me insane earlier."

Louise nodded, motioned for me to pass her the half-empty ketchup bottles so she could get to refilling them. "Must have been a heap of accidents. Heard there was a bunch of activity over by the old playground. Nobody around here can drive worth a good god-damn." Thomas snorted his agreement from the kitchen, and Louise turned to glance at him. "When's the last time we had snow in April? Seems like it's been ages."

"Right before Junie was born," I said without hesitation. "Thirteen years." I remembered how big I'd been, ankles swollen to the point I couldn't shove my feet into snow boots and had to navigate the drifts in my worn tennis shoes.

"Oh Lord, that's right," Louise said. She finished filling a ketchup bottle and slid it back down my direction. "You have big Saturday night plans?" She did a sideways shimmy. "Maybe a little dancing? A little drinking? A little something-something?"

"I promised Junie I'd be home early and we'd have pizza and

watch a movie. I haven't seen her since yesterday." I didn't need to see Louise's eye roll to know how pathetic she found my version of an exciting Saturday night. She'd already told me enough times that youth was wasted on me. *Thirty going on fifty* was one of her favorite commentaries on my nonexistent social life.

"When mine were that age, I'd a been happy if someone had taken them away for a week at a time. Little smart-asses." Louise shook her head. "Where's she been, anyway?"

"She stayed over with Izzy Logan." I kept my gaze on the swath of counter I was wiping. Ignored the pinch in the base of my skull.

"Those two are thick as thieves," Louise said, and I didn't miss the slight note of disbelief in her voice. I was used to it by now, understood that girls like Junie and girls like Izzy didn't usually run in the same crowd. Especially not in this town, which might as well have a neon strip painted down the middle. *Poor white trash on this side. Do not cross.* Didn't seem to matter that 90 percent of the town was stranded on the wrong side. The invisible line wasn't budging based on majority rule, at least not when it came to mixing with Jenny Logan's family. When I was in junior high, out searching the roadside ditches for cans I could recycle, I used to see Jenny tooling around in her little white convertible. She left for college when I was a sophomore in high school, and I'd assumed she was gone for good. But she'd returned two years later with half a degree she'd never used and a college boy groomed to take over her dad's boat dealership. They weren't anything special by city standards, but around here the Logans were practically royalty. It didn't take much. A decent job and a house that wasn't moveable usually did the trick.

"Yep," I said. I hated how everyone acted like I ought to be grateful that Izzy liked my daughter, that Izzy's parents welcomed Junie into their home. No one ever asked me what I thought, probably would have been surprised to discover that I wasn't grateful at all. That I would've put a stop to the friendship a long time ago if I could have figured out a way to do it without breaking my daughter's heart. I resented the phone calls from Jenny arranging get-togethers, always assuming, even after constant reminders to the contrary, that my schedule was endlessly flexible. I looked away from the perfunctory waves Izzy's father, Zach, gave from the front porch when I pulled up in my ancient Honda, the back window jury-rigged out of cardboard and duct tape. I kept waiting (and wishing) for the first bloom of friendship to fade, for some stupid drama to tear the girls apart. But it had been years now, and so far, the bond they had was made of stronger stuff. And I didn't like that, either. Hated thinking about what it might mean.

I dropped the rag on the counter and pressed my hands into my lower back. I was too young to feel like such shit at the end of the day, my legs aching and spine a dull throb. You would have thought the snow might've made for a quiet day at the diner, but weather was everyone's second-favorite topic, right behind politics. The place had been hopping all day, only now emptying out as everyone made their way home for dinner. The pie rack had been cleared out, and I didn't want to estimate how many cups of coffee I'd poured in the last eight hours. Lots of jawing and not a whole lot of tipping. My least favorite kind of day.

"Looks like your brother's pulling in," Louise said. "Hope he doesn't want a piece of apple. He's shit outta luck."

I straightened up, watched Cal's car slide to a stop out front. Even after all these years, the sight of my brother behind the wheel of a patrol car came as a little shock. We'd spent the majority of our childhoods evading the cops, grew up always keeping one eye out for the law. The kind of public service that might earn us an extra dollar from the dealers using our mama's cracked countertop as a storefront. So cop hadn't exactly been at the top of my list of promising potential professions for my brother. But he'd surprised me, first by becoming one and then turning out to be good at the job. Word around town was he was tough but always fair. Which was more than could be said for his boss and the other lazy-ass deputies. Once, when Thomas had spent a night in jail after he'd made a drunken mess of himself, he'd told me that Cal had "a real nice way about him, even when he was putting on the cuffs." Praise for the law didn't come higher than that, not around here.

"He's not usually in town on Saturdays," I said. The cops around here were spread thin, patrolling not just Barren Springs but multiple small towns and the long stretches of almost empty highway in between.

"Maybe the man needs a cup of coffee," Louise said. "I'm sure he's had a long day." She fluffed her hair with one hand. Louise was old enough to be Cal's mom and then some, but even she turned ridiculous in his presence, wanting to baby him and flirt with him in equal measure.

"Maybe," I said, but something heavy settled in my stomach as Cal unwound himself from the front seat of his cruiser. He shut the door and then stood there, head hanging down, dishwater-blond hair catching the light. After a moment, he straightened up, set his shoulders. Steeling himself, I thought, and the heavy knot in my stomach bottomed out through the floor. Those sirens . . . I told myself they had nothing to do with Junie, who was too young to drive and too old to be fooling around on a playground. I grabbed the rag and looked away from the window, went back to scrubbing at the cracked Formica countertop, didn't look up even when I heard the bell jangle over the door.

"Hey, Cal," Louise said, her voice pitched high and girlish. "You want—"

Out of the corner of my eye, I saw my brother hold up one hand, stopping Louise's voice in its tracks. "Eve," he said quietly, walking toward me. His cop shoes were loud on the ancient linoleum floor.

I didn't look up, kept scrubbing. Whatever he was here for, whatever had been nipping at me all day, it wouldn't be true, it wouldn't have *happened*, if I could keep him from saying it.

"Eve," he said again. I could see his belt buckle pressed up against the edge of the counter now, and he reached over, laid his hand on mine. "Evie . . ."

I jerked my hand away, took a step backward. "Don't," I said. I meant it to come out fierce and commanding enough to stop him from speaking, but my voice wobbled and broke, the single word dribbling away into nothing.

"Look at me," Cal said, gentle but firm. His big-brother voice. I raised my eyes slowly, not wanting to see, not wanting to know. Cal's eyes were red-rimmed and swollen. He'd been crying, I realized with a little electric jolt. I couldn't remember ever seeing Caleb cry, not once in our shitty shared childhood. I stared into his bright blue eyes, and he stared back. As always, it was like looking into a mirror, but one that threw my reflection back crisper and clearer. Same hair, same eyes, same smattering of freckles, but all of it overlaid with a sheen I simply didn't have. As if nature had blown its entire genetic wad on my brother, and when I came along eleven months later there was only enough left over for a faded, second-rate replica.

"What?" I said. Ready now, suddenly, for whatever hell was waiting for me behind his lips. When he didn't answer, I threw the rag at him, watching it slap into his chest and leave a wet stain against his shirt. "What?" I practically screamed. Louise moved up next to me and laid one hand on my forearm. Her touch, usually the closest thing I had to a mother's comfort, burrowed under my skin, and I jerked away, my whole body buzzing like a downed power line.

"It's Junie, Eve," Cal said. "It's Junie." His voice broke and he glanced away, his throat working. "You need to come with me."

I felt rooted to the spot, my feet sinking into the floor, my body heavy and leaden. "Is she dead?" Next to me Louise sucked in a sharp breath. That one sound letting me know that I'd gone a step too far, made a leap that Louise never would have. But Louise hadn't grown up the same way I had. No money, yeah. Food stamps and government cheese, yeah. But not violence. Not raised in a double-wide that stunk of random men and meth burners. Not strange faces and too much laughter, most of it jagged and mean. All of it nestled in the armpit of the Ozarks, a place only fifteen miles down the road, but so backwater, so hidden from the wider world, that it felt like its own dark pocket of time.

But Cal knew. He looked back at me, held my gaze. My brother never lied, not to me. Whatever came next would be the truth, whether I could stand it or not. "Yeah," he said finally. "She's gone. I'm sorry, Evie."

"How?" I heard myself say, voice far away like a helium balloon drifting above my head.

Cal's jaw tightened, and he sucked in a breath through his nose. "It looks like she was murdered." It wouldn't be until later, when I knew all the awful details, that I would remember this moment and realize how, even then, my brother was trying to spare me from something.

In my mind, I fell to the floor, mouth twisted and howling. Screamed my throat raw. Ripped out my own hair. Slammed face-first into the linoleum until my nose burst and dark blood flowed. But in reality, I simply turned and grabbed my coat and purse off the hook behind me, catching a single glimpse of Thomas's shocked face, his mouth open and eyes wide. Walked past Louise's out-stretched hand and around my brother's reaching arm. Pushed out into the cold, snow-scented air, squinted against the weak sunlight tearing through the clouds. It had happened now, finally. The disaster I'd been anticipating from the second Junie was born. And I had never even seen it coming.

TWO

It's never the thing you're expecting that wallops you. It's always something sneaky, sliding up behind you when your attention's fixed on something else. How many times had my mama told us that growing up? One tiny tidbit of valuable insight in her otherwise alcohol- and drug-fueled existence. The lesson learned from her own father, who suffered from a bum ticker, his every hiccup or wheeze a sure sign of impending death. Until the day stomach cancer crept up out of nowhere and snuffed him out before his heart knew what was happening. When I was a kid, my mama doled out wisdom so rarely that I clutched onto this nugget like a lifeline. Spent my time trying to foresee every single disaster that might befall us in hopes that nothing could catch us unawares. And when my daughter was born, I had anticipated a million ways my clawing, desperate love for her could go sideways: SIDS or choking on a piece of hot dog when Junie was little; a car accident or childhood leukemia as she grew; some dangerous older boy or her grandmother's taste for drugs reaching down through the generations now that she was approaching her teenage years. But her throat slit in the park where she'd played as a little girl? No, that was never a horror story I had entertained. Not in this small, middle-of-nowhere town, where if you didn't know someone you at least knew their kin, who they belonged to, where they came from. All of this was my fault, really. Because if I'd had a little more imagination, stolen the idea before the universe had grabbed on to it, maybe my girl would still be alive.

"Where is she?" I asked, head resting against the passenger window. Outside the daylight was fading fast, leaving a streak of orange sunset burning behind the clouds. Buildings blurred past as we drove down the pitted two-lane highway that served as the center of town: the general store with its uneven pyramid of toilet paper in the window, the whitewashed brick bank building turned a dirty gray over time, the sub shop where no one actually ate unless they wanted to flirt with food poisoning. How was I still here, in this forgotten, dead-end place that couldn't even boast of nostalgic charm? No quaint town square, no sidewalks to stroll down on spring days, no vintage shops selling handmade treasures, only a random collection of dilapidated buildings spread along the edge of the highway and a tired, dirty sameness to everyone and everything. Why hadn't I left and taken Junie with me? What had I been waiting for? Something rose up in my throat, vomit or tears, but I swallowed it down. *Not now*, I told myself. *Later.*

"She's at the funeral home," Cal said, eyes on the road, hands gripping the wheel with white knuckles. He paused, then gave it to me straight, the way he always had. "Waiting for the medical examiner. They both are."

He'd already told me Izzy was dead, too, and I was working hard to wrap my mind around it. How two twelve-year-old girls could be alive and laughing this morning and not breathing a few hours later. It was a cliché that they'd had their whole lives ahead of them, but it had also been the truth. I didn't understand how my daughter, whose presence lit up a room, whose life made mine bearable, could be dead. Shouldn't the world have stopped spinning the moment she left it?

Cal pulled up right in front of the funeral home, in the space usually reserved for the hearse. The entrance was flanked with faux pillars in an attempt to give the place a distinguished air and distract from the fact it was a crappy cinder block building set on a cracked asphalt lot. Not the kind of place anyone would choose to say their final good-byes. Cal turned off the engine, the early evening suddenly bathed in quiet. When he turned to look at me, his face was pale and grim. "Can you do this?" he asked. "Because you don't have to. Not right now."

But I was already pushing out of the passenger side. "I can do it," I said over my shoulder. Truth was, I didn't know if I could. But moving forward felt like my only option. Sitting still would kill me, would give reality a chance to settle down beside me and sink its teeth in, all the way to the bone. I didn't want to contemplate, even for a second, my life without Junie in it. How empty it would be from now on. How pointless.

There was another deputy waiting for us just inside the door, hat held in front of his beer-habit belly. John Miller, who I'd known my whole life, who'd let me sit in the back of his squad car to keep warm when the cops had showed up to search my mama's trailer for meth. Once a year like clockwork and always drove away empty-handed. My mama may have been ignorant, but she was never, ever stupid. But today Deputy Miller acted like he'd never seen me before, said "Sure am sorry" in a low voice, and kept his gaze somewhere to the left of my shoulder. It didn't bother me any, even though I could feel Cal stiffening up next to me. I didn't want to look into Miller's eyes, either, to see the pity and horror there. Wanted to keep pretending this was a particularly lucid nightmare I'd wake up and tell Junie about, snuggled with her on her narrow bed. I'd hug her too tight and she'd squirm away, telling me not to worry.

"Sheriff's waiting for you on back in the bereavement room," Miller said, clapped one hand on Cal's shoulder as we walked past. I stumbled a little, small enough that no one else would have noticed, but Cal put out a hand, gripped me around the elbow. "It's okay," he murmured. "We're all on the same team now."

Sheriff Land and I would never be on the same team, not if we both lived for a thousand years. But I couldn't tell Cal that, couldn't ever look him in the eye and explain why. If he knew what I'd done, he'd never forgive me. And even worse, he'd never forgive himself. I nodded and followed him toward a closed door at the end of the hall. Cal hesitated with the knob in his hand, my last chance to back out, and then pushed the door open when I motioned him forward. He stood aside so I could go in first. The room was small, overheated, and crowded with too many bodies, even though there were only three already inside. Sheriff Land and Izzy's parents, Jenny and Zach. I don't know why their presence surprised me. Maybe the realization that we were going to be a matched, albeit uneven, set from now on. The parents of the dead girls. Forever lumped together. Pitiful cautionary tales.

"Come on in," Sheriff Land said, oversized gray mustache quivering on his lip. His hair was slicked back, covering the beginning of a bald patch I knew had to be killing him. My stomach cramped and I looked away. "Take a seat." And a beat too late, "Hate that you have to be here," as if he was only now remembering why I was in the room. As if the fact that I had a murdered daughter, too, had somehow slipped his mind.

I slid into the empty seat next to Zach, who gave me a quick glance with wide, shocky eyes. His bland dad handsomeness had morphed into something terrible, and I wondered if I was just as altered. If I would no longer recognize myself next time I looked in the mirror. He had the same button-down shirt and khaki pants, straight teeth and premature gray at his temples, that I was used to seeing. But his face was haunted now, the ghost of his daughter's absence etched across his features. On the other side of him, Jenny wept ceaselessly. All I could see was the top of her sleek, dark hair, her head tilted down and her sobbing muffled behind a clump of sodden Kleenex. From the soft way Sheriff Land looked at her, I could tell that Jenny, at least, had gotten the grieving-mother role exactly right. Not like me, who couldn't seem to lay a hand on my own tears yet, but felt them bottled up and howling just behind my eyes.

Sheriff Land took the seat across from us, pushing a dusty arrangement of fake flowers to the side to give himself an unimpeded view. Cal took up a position leaning against the wall, arms folded across his chest. "Well, now," Sheriff Land said, "I know this is difficult. And I sure do hate to ask you folks questions at a time like this, but the more we know and the earlier we know it, the better our chances of catching this guy."

"You know it's a guy?" I asked, hands knotting on the tabletop.

Sheriff Land paused. "We don't know anything for certain at this point. But this kind of crime, the way they were killed . . ." He shook his head. "Be unusual for a woman, that's all."

I thought that was the dumbest thing I'd ever heard. Women might not act out as often as men, but they were capable of anything, could be as awful and vicious as men when they wanted to be. I knew firsthand the violence that could live inside women. "Were they raped?" I asked. "Is that why you're sure it was a man?" Land's face tightened up. He didn't like my talking, interrupting the picture of how this was going to go that he'd already worked out inside his own head. Sheriff Land loved being in control, making everyone dangle on his string. On the other side of Zach, Jenny sucked in a breath, a low moan escaping on her exhale. Zach reached over and patted Jenny's arm, shot me a warning look that took me by surprise.

"What?" I said. "Am I not supposed to ask things like that? Are there *rules* in this situation that I'm not aware of?" Anger simmered inside me, anger I'd been careful with for years. Not wanting to give anyone a reason to look down on my daughter. But now it didn't matter anymore. Didn't matter if I was a smart-ass or got in fights or acted a fool. Junie was gone and I could let it all spill out. I couldn't think of a better place to start than right here in this room.

Land cleared his throat, glanced over his shoulder at Cal.

"No," Cal said from his spot against the wall. "No rules." He caught my gaze, held it. "We won't know anything for certain until the medical examiner gets here. But from what we can tell, it doesn't look like they were raped. Clothes were intact."

I nodded, looked at Land, and waited for him to continue.

"We're wondering if the girls talked about anybody new lately? Someone they'd met? Anything different with their routines? Demeanors? Anything stand out to you folks at all?"

I scrolled through the last few weeks, searching the corridors of my own memory and coming up with nothing. "I can't think of anything," I said finally. "Junie seemed like her regular self."

"Izzy was fine, too," Zach said, his voice hoarse with tears. "As far as I know."

We all looked at Jenny, who nodded her agreement. "I don't understand," she said, from behind her fistful of tissues. "It was a stranger, wasn't it? I mean, someone from another place? No one from *here* would do something like this."

Spoken like the unofficial ambassador of Barren Springs, I thought. Even now defending the reputation of a town that didn't deserve it. "Well, now," Sheriff Land said, "we don't get a lot of tourists or out-of-towners this time of year. We're not assuming anything, but we've got to take a look at local folks, too."

Truth be told, we didn't get many tourists or out-of-towners any time of year, unless you counted people stopping for a tank of gas on their way to greener pastures. Generally someplace closer to one of the lakes that drew people to this part of the world in the first place. And I seriously doubted those people would know how to find the dilapidated town park or be interested in going there in the middle of a snowstorm. Land might not be ready to assume anything, but I sure as hell was. My daughter and Izzy had been killed by someone local, someone whose face they probably recognized. Something ached deep down in my gut, and I wasn't sure if my daughter knowing the person who'd taken her life made Junie's last moments better or worse.

"All right," Land said, leaning back in his chair, hands steepled on the table in front of him. "What about people hanging around the girls? Notice anyone driving by your houses? Maybe the same face showing up when you were out?" He looked from me to Zach and then Jenny. "Nothing like that?"

"This town has less than a thousand people," I pointed out. "I see a lot of the same people over and over." I flicked a hand toward Zach and Jenny. "They probably do, too." I knew my attitude wasn't helping, wasn't doing the hunt for Junie's killer any favors. But I didn't know how to sit across from Land and act like we were anything less than adversaries. Our roles had been written in stone a long time ago.

Land sighed. "All right, then. What about Jimmy Ray? You seen him lately?"

I stared at Land, our gazes locked. "No," I said, voice even. "I haven't seen him." I paused. "Have you?"

Land's brow furrowed. "Now, listen—"

"Who's Jimmy Ray?" Zach asked. "Did he have something do to with this?" This question, more than anything else he could have said, cemented Zach's status as an outsider. It didn't matter that he'd lived in Barren Springs for more than a decade, volunteered with the fire department, and had married Jenny Sable. If you were born in this town, if you really belonged, you knew everyone else. Simple as that.

"He's just a local loser," Jenny said, nose stuffy. "Jimmy Ray Fulton. You'd know him if you saw him. He's got the truck with the loud muffler you always complain about."

"Jimmy Ray's her ex," Land said, hooking his thumb at me without bothering to glance my way. "Runs a meth operation her mama's a part of."

"Ex-boyfriend, not husband," Cal supplied, as if that distinction was going to make a damn bit of difference to the Logans.

"Meth?" Zach said, like he'd never heard the word before. "Did he say meth?" His eyes skated around the room looking for an answer.

"Yeah," I said. "Meth. You know, this part of the world's little cottage industry. Or at least it used to be. I've heard Jimmy Ray's branching out into heroin these days. Going after the serious money. That what you hear, too, Sheriff?" I swung my gaze to Land. From the corner of my eye I could see Cal staring at me, could imagine the look on his face. *Who is this smart-mouth woman? Where has she been hiding all these years? I thought she was gone for good.* I, for one, was relieved she'd made a reappearance. The Junie's-mom version of me wasn't going to make it through this. But maybe the old, hard-edged Eve Taggert had a shot at surviving.

"I don't understand," Jenny said. She looked from me to Land. "You think Junie's father might have had something to do with this?" I could hear the accusation in her voice, and underneath it the total lack of surprise. No one would want to hurt Izzy, no animal who would cut a girl's throat was part of the Logans' neat and tidy lives. So it had to be Junie. She'd brought this on their daughter, not the other way around. The worst part was I thought Jenny was probably right.

"Jimmy Ray's not her father," I said, voice hard. "And he wasn't involved. Even he has standards." Honestly, I had some doubt about Jimmy Ray's standards, or lack thereof, but I needed to believe he wasn't capable of something like this.

For a moment no one spoke, the buzz from the fluorescent lights like a jackhammer inside my head. "What about her actual father, then?" Land said finally. "What's his story? Could he have been involved?"

"No," I said, nothing more.

"He live around here?" Land pressed.

I sighed, knew he was doing this for the benefit of the Logans. Land was already well aware of my status as a tried-and-true single mother. "Nope," I said. "It was one time. He was passing through town. A fuck-and-run, I think they call it." Zach stiffened up next to me, and I felt a cheap thrill at having shocked him.

"Never saw him again?" Land said.

Memories of that single night flashed through my mind: dark, tousled hair and big-city dreams; equal parts wild and sweet and my back scraped raw on the edge of the diner's countertop; the hand he'd laid on my cheek before he drove away. I pushed the memories back where they belonged. "I haven't laid eyes on him since that night."

Land nodded, looked down at the notebook in front of him, but not before I saw the gleam of satisfaction in his gaze. But if he was hoping to humiliate me, he'd have to do a lot better than that. *He already has*, my mind whispered, and now it was my turn to look away.

"Can you walk me through this morning?" he said, glancing at Jenny. "What time did the girls leave your house?"

Jenny worried her hands together, took a shaky breath. "Um . . . Junie was planning on going home after lunch. Early afternoon." She glanced at me. "I made them grilled cheese sandwiches and tomato soup around one, and then Junie packed up her things. I was going to drive her home, but Izzy begged me to let them walk. They wanted to play in the snow." She swiped at her wet cheek with one hand. "They were only twelve," she whispered. "They just wanted to walk in the snow."

Zach put one arm around her shoulder, and she leaned her head against him. Her voice was slightly muffled as she continued, "Izzy was going to call me as soon as they got to Junie's, and I would drive over and pick her up. But instead the police showed up at our door."

"The park's not on the way to Eve's apartment," Cal pointed out.

"No," Jenny said. "It's not. I don't know why they were there."

Calling it a park was really nothing more than wishful thinking. A couple of swings, a cracked cement tunnel usually filled with dead leaves and cat shit. An old wooden seesaw studded with splinters. The elementary school next door had been torn down before I was born, and all that remained was the neglected playground, surrounded by a rusted chain-link fence. Junie and I went probably once a year, and I always swore to myself we wouldn't return. It was a sad excuse for a park, one that left you feeling depressed rather than carefree. But if you wanted the chance to push your child on a swing in Barren Springs, it was your only option.

Land pointed one finger at me. "You work a full shift at the diner today?"

I nodded. "Eight thirty to five."

"What about you, Zach? Were you at work today?"

"Yeah. Left this morning around eight. Spent the whole day at the dealership. I was still there when you all showed up."

"Take a lunch break or anything?" Land asked, eyes on his notebook.

Zach paused, and his arm jerked next to mine the moment he caught up. "You think one of *us* might have done this?"

Land gave a small shrug, held up both hands. "Of course I don't. But I have to dot all my i's and cross all my t's. That's the way these investigations work."

I snuck a glance at Zach, saw the muscle in his jaw jumping. "I took a twenty-minute lunch break. Late, around two. Went down the road and grabbed a sandwich."

That took him off the hook, assuming he was telling the truth. The boat dealership was a good thirty minutes away, in the next town along the highway. One with a Dollar General and a McDonald's and an actual library, small as it was. There was no way Zach could have gotten from there to here, killed two girls, and gotten back in twenty minutes. Not that I'd actually entertained the idea he might have done it. But still, it was good to check his name off the list in my head.

"And what about you?" Land asked, turning to Jenny.

"I was home all day," Jenny said. She still seemed confused about why he was asking. Surely he didn't think *she* could have done this awful thing.

"Didn't go anywhere after the girls left?"

"No."

I leaned around Zach to look at her. "I tried to call you around three. You didn't answer."

Jenny blinked at me. Her eyes were big and brown and protruded a little, like some kind of innocent woodland creature. "I . . . I was home. Maybe I was doing laundry? The dryer can be loud." She looked from me to Zach and back again.

"Why did you call her?" Land asked me.

"To check on Junie. She doesn't . . ." I paused, sucked in a breath. "Didn't have a cell phone. I wanted to make sure she was going to be home by five."

"Did you leave a message?" Zach asked, voice hard, like I was the one with something to hide.

"No," I said. "I was planning to call back later, but I got busy."

"What about Izzy?" Land asked. "She got a cell phone?"

Zach nodded. "My old iPhone. A 5 or a 6."

"A 6s," Jenny said. "Black. It's got a crack in one corner of the screen. A pink glitter case. Did you find it?"

Land didn't answer, scrawled something on his notepad.

Jenny shifted back in her chair. The legs caught on the nappy carpet, and she pitched forward as she tried to stand. She put one hand on the table to steady herself. "I need to go home," she said. "I can't do this right now. Please. I've had enough."

The second the words were out of her mouth, Land was standing, saying, "Sure, sure, we can talk more tomorrow." Somehow I was pretty sure if I'd been the one asking for an end to the conversation, Land would have found a way to put me off, telling me only a few more questions, we'd be done soon.

I stayed seated as Jenny and Zach shuffled out behind me, no one meeting anyone's eyes. I waited until they were out in the hall, Land shaking both their hands and patting Jenny on the shoulder, before I looked at Cal.

"You ready to go?" he asked.

"No," I said. "I want to see her."

THREE

No, you don't," Cal said, quick as a whip. "Evie, trust me. You don't."

"I do," I said.

Cal pushed off the wall, came toward me with hands outstretched. "Okay, well, at least wait until . . . after. When the funeral people have her cleaned up. Not now."

"Now," I said. "I need to, Cal. I *have* to."

"It's her, if that's what you're worried about," Cal said. "I saw her. It's Junie."

I shook my head. It wasn't that. I didn't doubt that Junie was gone. Already I could feel a gaping hole in the world where she used to be. But I needed to see, to be a witness to what had happened to my daughter. I couldn't live the rest of my life and not know, go on without having seen it with my own eyes. Junie had endured so much. The least I could do for her was endure this. "Let me see her, Cal." That stubborn set to my voice that Cal had heard a hundred times before and knew better than to argue against. "I'm not leaving until you do."

The bodies were down in the basement, in the embalming room. Cal and Land led me down the steps, the smell of formaldehyde hitting me in the face the second they pushed through the door into the hallway. It reminded me of high school biology, slimy frogs, split open and flayed, organs shimmering under too-bright lights. My vision swam, and I sucked in a deep breath through my nose, let it out slowly through my mouth.

"You sure you want to do this?" Land asked, eyebrows raised. "I'd advise against it." He hitched his pants up. "I've seen a lot of bodies in my day, and once you see 'em, you can't unsee 'em."

I barely glanced at him. "I'm sure."

"Always were a stubborn one," Land muttered under his breath, but waved me forward to where Cal was standing next to a set of swinging doors. "Don't touch her." Land pointed at me. "Not at all. I'm gonna watch through the window just to make sure."

"You want me to go in with you?" Cal asked, but I shook my head. "All right, then," he said. "She's on the left." He laid a hand on my back. "I'll be waiting right out here."

The door swung closed behind me, and I paused, took in the cracked linoleum floor with a drain in the center, the rolling cart I assumed held instruments no one wanted me to see because it had been haphazardly draped with a cloth, the same flickering fluorescent lights as the hallway. And two rolling stretchers in front of me, one on the left, one on the right, the bodies still encased in black body bags, although the one on the left had been unzipped.

I stared at the points of Junie's toes sticking up from the open body bag. Wondered, fleetingly, if she'd lost her shoes somewhere along the way or if they'd taken them off of her once she got here. Keeping my eyes on the lower half of her body, I moved up next to her, let my hand hover over her arm. I could feel the coldness radiating off her. My girl, who always ran hot, even on the most frigid days.

"This isn't fair," I said, voice low and choked. But it was a stupid thing to say, a worthless lament. Life was never fair. I knew that better than anyone. I took a deep breath, steeled myself, and then raised my eyes slowly upward, girding myself one inch at a time. But it wasn't as terrible as I'd expected, because it wasn't really my daughter lying there. My daughter—who loved pasta and the color yellow, who was prone to headaches and worried her legs were too long, who snorted when she laughed and hated her freckles—wasn't there anymore. This was the shell of a girl, one I hardly recognized as my own. Chestnut hair matted with blood, face chalky white from the nose up, a red horror below. Blood smeared across her chin and caked on her left cheek, her shirt soaked black. Her throat was laid open, almost ear to ear.

I had been the first person to hold her when she came into the world. I witnessed her first word, her first steps, her first fever, laugh, tantrum, crush, disappointment. But not this. Her last breath, her final seconds on earth. I wasn't there in the moment when she needed me the most. All my years of trying hadn't mattered because in the end, I had failed her. I leaned forward and kissed the air above her unmarred forehead. I breathed in, hoping for some last remnant of her. But all I could smell was blood and new-fallen snow.

. . .

Cal wouldn't let me spend the night alone, trudged after me up the cracked sidewalk to my apartment building, even when I told him I was fine (a lie so pathetic, neither one of us acknowledged it), that I wanted to be alone, to please go home. Most of the outside lights on my building had long since burned out, and repeated calls to the manager hadn't produced anything other than half-hearted promises to come check it out. The only illumination was from the lone streetlight in the parking lot, but it was enough for me to spy a plate of something left on my front doormat. Word traveled fast around here. Heart-shaped cookies, it turned out, each one frosted in pale pink. More appropriate for the birth of a daughter than the death of one. I kicked the plate out of the way, cookies sailing out onto the cigarette-butt-littered concrete.

"Hey," Cal said, and then seemed to think better of it, his voice trailing off into silence.

The apartment looked the same as when I'd walked out this morning, and completely forever changed at the same time. It had always been the apartment of a family who only escaped true poverty through sheer stubbornness and the generosity of others. Others being Cal, who bought my groceries half the time and made sure the electricity was never shut off. But the shabbiness felt new to me. The lumpy brown sofa and nicked dining table. The thin curtains and scuffed paint. Had it always looked this threadbare and colorless? This empty? *Of course it hasn't*, my mind whispered. *Because Junie used to be here.* Filling it up with her sound and her voice and her smells. Junie, who was never going to be here again.

Cal made a noise behind me, something deep and guttural, and I spun, my heart hammering in my throat. He'd slid down onto the floor, his back against the now-closed front door, hands held out in front of him, cupping something invisible.

"Remember when she was born?" he asked. He didn't take his eyes from his hands, couldn't see me nod. *Of course I do*, I wanted to shout. *How could I ever forget?* But I reminded myself that he was grieving, too. That although the loss of Junie was something I wanted to clutch tight in my palm, whisper *mine* through bared teeth, such selfishness would be unfair. She loved Cal, and he loved her. He had a right to his sorrow, but I couldn't find room inside myself to care about his pain. Not now. Not yet. "She fit right here," he said, lifting his palms. "She was *tiny*. I mean, I'd seen babies before, but not like that. Not so *new* and small and fragile."

I'd had the same thoughts the first time I'd held her. I'd wanted to roll her into a ball and pop her into my mouth, swallow her back down into my belly, where she'd been protected. Keep her there, where I could stand between her and the world's shadows. Maybe somehow I'd known, even then, what was waiting for her. Or maybe I just didn't know how to hope for the best. God knows I'd never been taught.

"I told her I was her Uncle Cal and she was my Junie-bug. I'd always love her and I'd always take care of her." He paused, a sob sliding out of his mouth. "I promised her she'd always be safe."

"You did take care of her," I managed. "You kept her safe."

"Before." His hands dropped to his sides. "But then today came along and made a liar out of me."

And what could I say to that? We hadn't kept her safe and there was no arguing the fact. Junie's split-open body was the undeniable proof. "Are you going to find out who did it? Are you going to catch him?" I paused. "Or her?"

Cal looked at me, and I saw the truth swirling in his tear-bright eyes. This is a slippery part of the world. People dart in and out of existence like minnows in a shadowy pool. It's not uncommon for someone to show up in town who everyone thought was dead, it's been so long since they've been around. Folks here are hard to pin down, even harder to catch. The land itself serves as its own kind of hiding place, full of nooks and valleys, tucked-away places where no one would ever think to look. It's a place for people who don't want to be found. But Cal nodded. "Yeah. Sure. Of course. We'll get him." The vow came too fast, too easily. The kind of promise it's easy to make because you've already broken it before the words are even spoken.

It was the first time he'd ever lied to me.

. . .

Cal woke me in the morning, bright sun streaming in from behind my pale curtains. "What time is it?" I muttered, putting one hand over my aching eyes. I still hadn't cried, not a single tear, and my lids throbbed. My whole face felt swollen with unshed grief, like an overfilled balloon waiting to pop.

"Almost eight," Cal said, holding out a mug of coffee that I waved away. "I called and talked to Thomas, told him you wouldn't be in for a while."

I shoved myself up onto my elbows. "I can't miss work."

Cal shook his head. "I'll cover you if you need some money. Thomas said he'd help, too. You can't go to work, Evie. Come on, you know that."

He was right, of course. I could imagine what a mood killer I'd be. No one wanted to eat pie and shoot the shit with a murdered girl's mother hovering around, eyes red-rimmed and soul cut out.

"I've gotta go in, though," Cal said. "But I'll come back tonight."

He paused, looked away. "Can I trust you alone?" he asked quietly. "Trust you not to do anything crazy?"

"Are you asking me if I'm going to kill myself?" I asked, voice even. I waited until he looked at me, his brow knotted up with worry. "No," I said. "I won't do anything crazy. Not today." That's all I could give him. One day. I didn't know about tomorrow. I was done making promises. I'd made Junie a thousand and not one of them had mattered in the end.

"Okay," Cal said, blowing out a breath. He kissed my cheek and set the mug on my bedside table. "I left the sheets and blankets on the sofa," he said from the doorway. "I'm staying here again tonight. I love you."

"I love you, too," I told him. "Always."

After he left, I burrowed back under the covers, breathed in my own unwashed smell. Closed my eyes and sank into oblivion. Going, going. Gone.

.   .   .

Three days passed before I got out of bed for more than a trip to the toilet. Three days where the only person I talked to was Cal and one quick call with the funeral director. Cremation, I told him. Plain urn. No funeral. He paused after that last instruction, cleared his throat. Asked me to repeat. "No funeral," I said again, louder. Later, when Cal walked through the door, I knew the two of them had talked.

"I heard you don't want a funeral," he said. He put a plate with a grilled cheese sandwich and a small bunch of grapes on my bedside table. Picked up the one holding a blueberry muffin, uneaten, that he'd put there this morning. I wasn't sure why he was bothering.

"I don't want a funeral," I confirmed.

31

Cal sat on the edge of my bed, slid his fingers through my greasy, matted hair. "Evie, honey, a funeral is everyone's chance to say good-bye. To celebrate Junie's life."

"She didn't have a life," I told him. "She lived twelve years. That's it. Twelve." The number sounded even worse out loud. Twelve summers, twelve Christmases, twelve trips around the sun. It was nothing in the scheme of things. Nothing.

"She had a life," Cal said. "She lived."

I shrugged out from under his hand, turned away. "I didn't say never. I said not now."

"What are you waiting for?"

To know who did it. To say good-bye to my daughter with at least the knowledge that whoever killed her wasn't still walking around, thinking they got away with it. "I'm not sure. But when the time is right, I'll let you know."

FOUR

The next morning I waited until Cal was gone and then I unfurled from my cocoon. My legs were weak from being in bed for days. I stunk of sweat, and there were purple bruises under my eyes even though all I'd done for three days was sleep. I didn't want to move, but grief was a luxury I couldn't wallow in forever. I stood under a scalding-hot shower until my skin turned a bright lobster pink, and I scrubbed at my hair until my scalp screamed.

The day was bright and sunny, as every day had been since the snowstorm. As if nature were trying to make amends for her colossal fuckup. My eyes protested the light, and I slipped on a pair of sunglasses, slid behind the wheel of my car, which Thomas had dropped off a few days ago. I sat with my hands on the steering wheel, feeling like I did at fourteen when I first learned to drive.

Confused and unsure about how it all worked. It seemed unfathomable that I had been driving around town just a week ago, everything normal, Junie next to me fiddling with the radio, her feet forever propped up even when I told her a thousand times to put them down. If I peered closely enough, I could still see the outline of her tennis shoe on the dash.

I bent down and pressed my forehead against the steering wheel, hard enough to leave a mark. Hard enough to push the memories back where they belonged. I needed to be in control. The place I was going didn't allow for weakness.

It was only fifteen miles to my mom's trailer, but it took more than forty minutes to make the trip. The last five miles over terrain that could only be loosely termed an actual road. Dirt and pitted gravel, not featured on any Google map or adorned with a single road sign. What little mail my mom got was picked up at a post office box in town. She didn't have an actual address. Growing up, I didn't know a single person who did. Locations were given in terms of landmarks and miles traveled: *Take the first right at the rusted pickup; head south for about a mile; veer left at the gravel fork in the road; if you pass a burned-out double-wide, you've gone too far.*

"Damn it," I whispered over and over again as my car slammed against the rough road. I was getting close now, and tension curled between my shoulder blades, stretched its talons up into my neck. A headache throbbed behind my eyes. To the right I saw Carl Swanson's trailer, one end completely rotted off, the hole patched with a tattered tarp and ribbons of duct tape. There was a new sign in his yard, black paint on an old piece of plywood. *Rabbits $2.* The greasy taste of rabbit rose in my throat, even though it had been years since I'd eaten one. Around here rabbits weren't sold as pets, to be cuddled and loved by small children. They were meat, cheap and readily available. Chopped up in stew, legs boiled on the stove, stringy gray meat slopped over plates of gummy rice.

I glanced to the left, looking at the view where the land dropped off, a valley of ripening green stretching out, dotted with old-growth woods, a glint of silver reflecting off the river snaking through. I'd seen it a thousand times—from winter bare to summer lush—but the view never got old. The kind of unblemished beauty that tethered people to this part of the world. Nature that still felt untouched and pure. It was this exact valley, apparently, that had given Barren Springs its name. As the legend went, when the first settlers found this place, there was only one almost-dry little creek and a bunch of dead trees. Soil too hard and rocky to grow much of anything but weeds. But the settlers were tired, out of provisions and choices. So they stayed. And prayed. Begged the Lord to bless them any way he saw fit, but, hey, some water, plentiful game, and better land would be a nice start. Beat their breasts and wept and gave it all up to God. Woke up the next morning to this green abundance. Rivers and creeks flowing, woods full of animals, soil still crap, but beggars can't be choosers, and two out of three ain't bad. They decided to name this place Barren Springs to remind themselves how easily things could go bad and how God answered prayers if you truly believed. Most of the town had been praying to God ever since with crappier and crappier results, as far as I could see. For her part, my mama always subscribed to the theory that the settlers were such dumb shits they mistook a simple change of seasons for divine intervention.

I navigated around the bend in the road, slowing down in deference to potholes big enough to swallow a tire. Small rocks pinged off the undercarriage of my car, and my heart began its slow ascent into my throat. One more curve in the road that was really more of a track at this point, and my mother's trailer appeared. It was set back slightly from the road, ringed by tall grass and heaps of trash, old tires, and a rusted-out car that has been there for as long as I had memories. I used to hide in the footwell when things inside the trailer got too bad.

I bumped over the uneven ground and parked in the grass, next to a black pickup truck with a dented passenger door. Not my mama's. My stomach cramped up at the thought she had company. The people my mother invited inside were never people you wanted to meet. But my mama was sitting on the front steps of her trailer alone, a beer can in one hand and a cigarette in the other. She stared at me as I unfolded myself from the car, took a long drag off her cigarette as I approached.

My mama was sixteen when Cal was born. Seventeen when I came along, a year younger than I'd been when I brought Junie into the world. She'd almost died from a bad infection after my birth and there were no more kids after me, a fact she always brought up when she was drunk and angry. As if not being able to have more kids she couldn't afford and didn't want to take care of was the great tragedy of her life. She was forty-seven now, but looked sixty. Lank dishwater hair, summer-sky eyes, skinny arms and legs framing a loose pouch of belly and saggy breasts. Rumor was she'd been pretty once, maybe even beautiful. Her face the wellspring of Cal's own good looks. Had men panting around behind her until they figured out her wild streak wasn't the sassy-comeback type of attitude they saw in the movies. Mama's wild streak could tear you limb from limb. Even now, with skin dull and pockmarked from too much alcohol and too many drugs, her eyes were sharp. Watchful. She was a woman you underestimated at your own peril.

"Hey, Mama," I said.

She took another drag off her cigarette, blew the smoke in my direction.

"Hey, yourself."

I waited for her to say something about Junie, some acknowledgment of what had happened, and realized she was waiting for the same thing. "Cal called you," I said, more a statement than a question.

"Yep," she replied, and after another drag from her cigarette, "Sorry about it."

I sucked in a breath, looked away. The rear of the trailer had a big uneven gash in the siding. My mama had stuffed the tear with plastic bags and newspaper, but it probably did next to nothing to keep the cold out. I hadn't been inside the trailer in years, but could still picture every inch of it. Could probably navigate it blind, if I had to. Dark and dank, ratty brown carpet, food-encrusted dishes piled in the sink, faint smell of urine from the busted pipe in the bathroom. And always some man who'd be gone in a few months. Not that we ever wanted them to stick around any longer. As daddy candidates, they'd all left something to be desired.

"What?" my mama demanded, drawing my attention back to her. "What else do you want me to say? I didn't even know the girl. Every time I spotted you in town, you practically dragged her across the road to get away from me. You never would bring her around here." Something flashed in her eyes, some emotion that didn't quite match her words, but she looked away before I could catch hold of it.

"To all this?" I threw out an arm. "You're damn right I didn't."

My mama tsked under her breath, held up her beer can, and shrugged when I shook my head. "Suit yourself," she said.

"Whose truck is that?" I asked. "Boyfriend of the month?" I glanced at the bumper, where a *Make America White Again* sticker was plastered up against *My Other Toy Has Tits*. "Looks like you've picked a real winner."

My mama's eyes narrowed as she leaned forward, poked me hard in the thigh with her bony knuckle. "Better watch your mouth," she said. "You ain't so grown I can't still beat your ass."

Fear slithered through me; defiance, too. A kind of muscle memory taking over, transporting me back to childhood, where I'd spent half my time trying to dodge her fists and the other half daring her to hit me again. Five minutes back in her presence and already I felt dirtier, harder, than I had when I drove up. Somewhere in the near distance a dog barked, a harsh, ugly sound, like he was swallowing nails. Even without seeing him, I could picture a flea-bitten, half-starved pit bull chained up in a muddy yard. That was the thing about this part of the world: You didn't have to actually see something to know exactly how it would play out.

"What did you come here for, anyway?" my mama asked. "You even gonna sit down?" She scooted over on the rickety plywood step. Her version of a peace offering. I hesitated and then lowered myself next to her. She smelled like old cigarettes and dirty hair.

"I was wondering where Jimmy Ray hangs out these days," I said, eyes on my ragged nails and torn-up cuticles. Working in the diner always had played hell on my hands. Junie used to put lotion on them before I went to bed, lulling me to sleep with the scent of lavender.

"Why you asking?" My mama paused, ground out her cigarette on the step between us. Lit another one before she spoke again. "You think he had something to do with what happened?"

"Not really," I said, praying it was the truth. I'd brought Jimmy Ray into our lives, led him right up to our doorstep. I wasn't sure how I'd manage to keep on living if he'd been the one to hurt Junie. "But Sheriff Land asked about him. Got me thinking is all."

"Sheriff Land." She snorted. "Why you listening to anything he has to say? That man's as worthless as tits on a nun."

I smiled at that, held out my hand for a drag off her cigarette. She rolled her eyes, but handed it over.

"You know where Jimmy Ray lives," she reminded me. "Why you asking me?"

"Yeah, but you know I can't just roll up there. Not if I want my head to stay attached to my body." Jimmy Ray's house, tucked even farther into the holler than my mama's, was more like a fortress. No one approached without an invitation. No one who wanted to keep breathing, at least. Truth was, I didn't care much about breathing anymore. But I was the only one who could speak for Junie. I didn't trust anyone else, not even Cal, to see this through, to follow this path to the dark place where it surely led.

My mama glanced at my hand. "Are you going to give that back or should I light another?"

"Light another," I said, holding the half-smoked cigarette out of her reach. I hadn't smoked a cigarette in more than a dozen years, and the nicotine rushed through me, leaving me light-headed.

She shook her head, lit up a fresh cigarette. "Jimmy Ray could be anywhere. But I hear he spends a lot of time at that titty bar down the way, on 50. You know the one?"

"Yeah," I said. "I know it." Grimy and dark and full of desperate women. Exactly the kind of place, and women, Jimmy Ray loved. I experimented with blowing a smoke ring, but netted only an amorphous cloud.

"What was she like?" my mama asked, her gaze fixed on the woods creeping up around the trailer as if the trees were anxious to reclaim the ground they'd lost. "Your girl?"

Her words pierced me, but for once I didn't think she was trying to be cruel. I flicked the cigarette away, watched it smoke on the dirty gravel at our feet. A bird cawed nearby, and another answered in the distance. "She was smart," I said. "So much smarter than the rest of us."

"Huh, guess that wouldn't be too hard." My mama bumped her shoulder gently against mine.

"She was curious about everything. She loved animals, could sob for days over every stray dog I wouldn't let her bring home. All the kids liked her, but she was picky about who she became friends with. Science was her favorite subject. She wanted to know how things worked. She wrote poetry. Kept it in a little notebook she carried around." My words were coming too fast, slopping out of my mouth like water from a broken faucet. "Her hair was prettier than mine, thicker. She had the same freckles across her nose." I ran my fingers over my face, surprised when they came away wet.

"She sounds like a special girl," my mama said. "Like you raised her the way you thought best."

"I tried," I choked out. "I tried hard to do better than you did. I read to her every night when she was little. I never hit her or ignored her. She always had enough to eat, even if it meant I went to bed hungry. I told her I loved her every day." A wail burst out of me. "But it wasn't enough. Cal and I are here, we're grown and alive, and my daughter is dead." I turned and looked at her. "After everything, you still did better than I did. Go ahead, I guess you can have the last laugh now."

She shook her head, her eyes soft in a way I barely recognized. "I'm not laughing." And that was the thing that undid me—not my daughter laid open on a stretcher, not Cal's voice beside my bed, a kindness from my mother. Shame washed through me. I hated that it was comfort from her that I needed in order to cry. She leaned over and pulled me toward her, and I fell into her lap, buried my face in the dirty denim of her jeans. She stroked my hair while I sobbed, her muffled voice murmuring bits of childhood songs.

She'd always been good at this, waiting until you'd about given up on her once and for all and then reaching out with a tender hand. It reminded me of the few times she'd read to me as a child, tucked me up against her body on the couch and gave different voices to the characters in the secondhand picture book I'd gotten for Christmas. Once, she even made me a mug of hot chocolate to sip while she read. Her rare affection an offering I never could resist, even when I knew better. Because her sweetness was always short-lived, always out of the blue, so you could never predict or count on it. And that made the rest of the hours and weeks and years that much worse. Because you knew she was capable of something more, something different. And you were left always hoping for it, waiting for that rarely glimpsed side of her to show itself. Never quite able to let go.

When I finally pushed myself upright, face swollen and tear-smeared, my mama looked at me. Set down her beer, tossed her cigarette to the side, and held my face between her thin hands. "You were a good mama," she said, stared at me until I gave a weak nod, and then tightened her fingers until I wanted to pull away, the edges of her sharp nails digging into my skin. "But the time for being good is over," she said. "The time for bawling and feeling sorry for yourself is over. Do you understand?" This time she didn't allow for nodding, didn't give me any room to move or look away. Her cigarette-smoke breath bathed my face and her ice-chip eyes cut into mine. "You're made of stronger stuff than that. You find him, Eve. Whoever did this. You find him. And you make him pay."

FIVE

An eye for an eye makes the whole world blind had never been one of my mama's mottos. Her version of justice was less forgiving, more Old Testament. An eye for an eye. Or maybe even a life for an eye. People knew not to mess with my mama. Not unless they wanted far worse than what they'd given. She'd been known to beat the shit out of men twice her size. Had no qualms with fighting dirty or going for the jugular. Once, she'd snatched a fist-sized patch of hair off a woman's head for calling us white trash. Her advice wasn't a surprise to me. It was why I'd gone, really. The information about Jimmy Ray just an afterthought. What I'd really wanted was a second opinion to echo the voice in the back of my head. Permission to follow my own worst urgings.

When I pulled up to my apartment, Cal was waiting for me on

the steps, bouncing his keys in his hand. "Where have you been?" he demanded.

"I went for a drive," I said. "I needed to get out."

He cocked his head at me. "Where did you go?" I could tell he suspected, but I didn't want to say. Cal's relationship with our mama was as tortured as mine, but in a completely different way. He had always been her favorite, her shining star, even when she was mocking him or making him feel small. And for his part, he loved her in a way I couldn't. A way that involved actually being a regular presence in her life. But he also knew her, wasn't blind to her many and varied faults. And he wouldn't want me around her right now, not when I was vulnerable to her brand of poison. But if I didn't admit where I'd been, I knew our mama wouldn't, either. She liked her secrets. Leverage was always more useful than honesty. Another one of her lessons I'd be wise to remember.

"Nowhere." I shrugged. "Just driving."

"I tried to call you. About ten times."

"Sorry," I said. "I turned my phone off." I held up my dark phone as evidence.

I could tell he wanted to press, but to his credit, he didn't. Probably scared he'd push me right over the edge. "I was worried," he said finally. "And you need to hurry up and change if we don't want to be late."

I stared at him and then down at my threadbare jeans and gray T-shirt. "Why do I need to change? Where are we going?"

He took a step closer to me, his face softening. "Izzy's funeral, remember? It starts in less than an hour."

"Oh, shit," I said. "Give me ten minutes."

I didn't have a black dress, or any dresses, for that matter. I pulled on a pair of black slacks, shiny and cheap, and changed my T-shirt for a plain white button-down blouse with yellowing deodorant stains in the armpits. I scraped my hair back into a ponytail. In the mirror I looked thin and exhausted, my freckles standing out against my pale skin. The scariest part was how easily I recognized myself. As if the woman who'd looked in this mirror every day for the past twelve years had been the imposter and this broken, dead-eyed version was the real me, the Eve who was always destined to reappear.

"People are gonna ask about Junie's funeral," Cal called from the living room as I was slipping on a pair of scuffed black pumps. "They don't understand why you're not having one. Think it's strange."

"I don't care what people think," I said. For so long, that had been all I cared about. Measuring every action, every word, every thought against how it might reflect back on Junie. It was a kind of relief not to have to worry about it. Nothing I did, or didn't do, could hurt her anymore.

The church parking lot was already full by the time we arrived, but I refused Cal's offer to drop me off out front. Small groups were clustered along the sidewalk, and I didn't want to stand there alone, have to nod and accept condolences and hugs. I wanted to be whisked inside like a criminal before anyone had time to notice me. Cal sat with me in the car parked a block down the road until everyone else had filtered inside, and we snuck in right as they were closing the doors for the service.

I couldn't remember the last time I'd been inside a church. My mama had the same opinion of religion that she did of the law— nothing good ever came from either one of them, and they both used fear to persuade fools to follow their rules. If she had indulged an urge to bring us closer to God, this bland Methodist chapel would have been her last choice. She would have taken us to one of the "churches" scattered throughout the holler, instead. The kind of place with dirt floors and snakebit parishioners speaking in tongues. Something with a little fire to it. Something with teeth.

I slid into one of the back pews before Cal could pull me forward, kept my head tilted down into the hymnal I'd opened on my lap. I was scared to look up, scared to see all the people filling the church. Scared of my own reaction. Because in a town this size, the person who'd killed Junie and Izzy was bound to be sitting right there among us. Praying and singing and crying as if they hadn't wielded the knife themselves. Slowly, I raised my head. Ran my eyes along the rows of mourners. Jack Pearson from the tire store, with the gaze that always followed young girls a little too close. Sally Nickels, who'd hated me since I'd slept with her boyfriend in tenth grade. Dave Colson, whose love affair with the bottle made him mean and unpredictable. It could have been any of them. It could have been none of them.

"Hey," Cal murmured. "Hey, breathe." He reached over and rubbed my back, his hand warm and rough through my shirt.

I looked back down, kept my eyes on the hymnal until my vision blurred. When I looked up again, Zach and Jenny were approaching their daughter's casket. It felt like the entire church was holding its breath, the only sound Jenny's hoarse sobbing. A mean, hateful part of me wondered if she ever stopped. Her shoulders hunched as she placed a hand on Izzy's closed (thank God) casket and Zach reached forward, supporting her. He whispered something into her ear and began to guide her gently away. Everyone else averted their eyes, dying to look but not wanting to be caught staring. But I stared, and Zach's gaze caught mine, his face pulled taut with grief. A bright shock of anger pulsed under my skin. Who was going to hold me up? Who was going to put their arms around me? Cal couldn't do it forever, that was asking too much of him, but who else was there? I jerked my eyes away.

When it was over, the last prayer voiced, the last hymn sung, I wanted to escape the same way I'd arrived. But Zach and Jenny were allowed to exit first, and then they lined up by the front door. A gauntlet we had to run before we were free. I had no idea what to say to them. *Sorry for your loss* sounded wrong considering I'd suffered the exact same misfortune. And I had no words of comfort, no real belief that someday our loss would no longer feel like a gaping wound or that our daughters were better off. The dead were gone and the world could be a nasty, festering place. And somehow, our daughters had gotten tangled in its ugliness. That was the only truth I knew. At least I was smart enough to know that saying it out loud wouldn't be helpful to anyone.

Zach and Jenny were standing together in the vestibule, arranged under a banner of silver foil balloons spelling out *IZZY* and attached to the floor with hot-pink ribbons. I wondered if the person responsible for them was the same one who'd left me the cookies. A thoughtful gesture turned macabre and ghoulish in actual execution.

I was still worrying over what to say when Jenny saved me, her social graces much more polished than mine. Turned out I didn't need to say a word. She swept me into her thin arms the second I approached. Her tearstained cheek pressed into mine, and her shuddering breath whispered past my ear.

I pulled back as gently as I could, gritting my teeth against the urge to shove her off of me. "The service was very nice," I managed.

Jenny's lip quivered as she tried to smile. "Thank you."

Zach laid his hand on my back and I flinched away, feeling surrounded, buried under their grief and good intentions when I was struggling to stay afloat myself. "Is there anything we can do for you?" he asked.

I shook my head without looking at either of them. The air in the vestibule was too warm, the heater pumping even though the temperature outside was spring mild, and a bead of sweat slithered down my spine. I swallowed down the lump forming in my throat. "No, I'm okay. You worry about yourselves." The words came out harsh, accusing rather than conciliatory.

"Come on," Cal said, grabbing my hand. "Let's get some air."

I pushed out through the heavy double doors, letting them swing shut on Cal's hurried good-byes. I gulped in the fresh air, early evening painting the sky with pink. This had always been Junie's favorite time of day, when the light turned hazy and the clouds sparkled.

When Cal dropped me off at home, it took ten minutes of convincing to get him to let me go in alone. "You have to be getting sick of my couch," I pointed out. "It's lumpy as hell." He didn't disagree, but started to open his door anyway.

"Seriously, Cal," I told him. "I'll be fine. I just need some time alone."

He turned and looked at me, and I held his gaze. "Nothing stupid, right?" he said.

I nodded. I knew he meant a bottle of pills or a razor. My head in the oven. What I was planning might have been even dumber. But I wasn't like Cal; I lied all the time. Had it down to a science. "Nothing stupid," I agreed.

SIX

The titty bar my mama had mentioned, the one where Jimmy Ray had been hanging out recently, was about ten miles down the road, situated a few feet off the highway and topped with a giant sign announcing *ADUL EN ER AINMEN*. I didn't know if some thief had a hankering for *T*s or if there had never been any to begin with, but the sign had looked the same for as long as I could remember. And if anyone was confused by the missing letters, the silhouettes of naked women painted on the boarded-up windows were a dead giveaway as to what went on inside.

I didn't doubt that this was Jimmy Ray's new watering hole. My mama's information was always good. But I didn't think Jimmy Ray was spending his time here looking at boobs. He had that crazy charisma particular to very bad men. He didn't need to stuff dollar bills in the G-string of some washed-up meth addict to get his rocks off. He had women lining up to do that for free. Which meant whatever he was doing here was business related. Money laundering or signing up mules, if I had to guess. And business always made Jimmy Ray more careful than usual. Meaner, too.

I'd be lying if I said I wasn't nervous, maybe even scared. I knew what Jimmy Ray was capable of when he felt cornered. My wrist still ached on rainy days, and every time I thought of him fear pulsed at the base of my spine, my legs wanting to run even when he was nowhere in sight. But scared wasn't going to stop me. Not now. What's the worst he could do? Kill me? The thought didn't even bother me all that much.

I'd only been inside the strip bar once before, back when Junie was an infant and I'd been desperate for some extra money. I'd gotten about five minutes into the interview—had been told that while blow jobs and hand jobs were fine, actual fucking had to be off premises, but hadn't yet been asked to peel off my top so the owner could ogle my milk-heavy breasts—when Cal had barreled through the front door and dragged me back outside. I'd screamed at him for interfering, for treating me like a baby, but inside I'd pulsed with relief. Standing on that beer-sticky stage night after night, letting glassy-eyed men flick my nipples when I leaned over to take their money, would've kept Junie fed in the short run but killed something inside me in the long term, something I needed in order to be a different kind of mother than my own.

I jerked down the rearview mirror and looked at myself in the dim light of the parking lot. I pulled out my ponytail holder and ran my fingers through my hair, pinched some color into my cheeks, slicked some sheer gloss onto my lips. Jimmy Ray, for all his bravado and bullshit, was a fairly simple guy. He liked his women pliable and pretty. I couldn't give him the first one, but I could bluff my way through the second.

The smell was the first thing that hit me when I pushed through the heavy door. Sweat and spilled beer. Something dank and musky that made you immediately think of sex. And not the good kind. The dirty, hopeless, borderline-mean kind. I paused inside the doorway, let my eyes adjust to the darkness. Cheap strobe lights blinked on the edges of the long narrow stage that extended out into the middle of the bar, studded at intervals with stripper poles where a couple of topless women slid along their lengths, gazes somewhere far away. Music pounded into my skull, way too loud for the relatively small space and even smaller crowd. A few men hunched on bar stools pulled up to the stage, slack gazes pinned on the women above them. A table of guys in the corner, one of whom was getting an unenthusiastic blow job from a middle-aged stripper wearing only high heels and a silver G-string. His friends watched, too bored to do more than stare, too turned on to look away.

On the other side of the room, a bartender lounged behind the bar talking to a couple of men nursing beers. No one seemed to have noticed my arrival, which meant Jimmy Ray probably wasn't here. Everyone lived on high alert when he was around. I was the only woman in the place other than the ones working, but I wasn't worried. I was used to places like this, even though they hadn't been part of my life in years. If nothing else, my childhood had taught me how to navigate the world's seedy underbelly.

"Hey, Sam," I said, sliding into the empty bar stool next to the man on the end. He turned and looked at me, his face breaking into a slow smile. I'd always liked Sam. Of all Jimmy Ray's hangers-on, he was the most human, with his scruffy beard and tiny paunch of belly. He'd always had the decency to look sorry, at least, after

Jimmy Ray had a go at me. Which is more than I could ever say for the rest of them, Jimmy Ray included.

"Well, look who the cat dragged in. Jesus, Eve. How you been?" At the last second, it hit him and his whole face shifted. "Oh God, sorry," he said. "I just . . . I forgot for a second. About your daughter. I didn't hear until yesterday."

"Junie," I said.

"Yeah, yeah," Sam said, snapping his fingers. "That's right. Junie." He glanced down at his beer. "Sure am sorry."

"Thanks," I said, watching the red flush work its way up his neck, visible even in the semidark.

"What can I get you?" the bartender asked. He stared at me without smiling.

"I'm good," I told him.

He shook his head. "Don't take up a seat at my bar unless you're gonna order something." I vaguely recognized him from my time with Jimmy Ray. Mark, Mike, some *M* name. Back then, he'd worn his brown hair in a buzz cut but it was longer now, gathered in a stubby ponytail at the nape of his neck. A single gold hoop glinted in his ear. I imagined a certain type of woman would find him attractive, one who took a quick look instead of paying attention to the details. Because he was the kind of good-looking that didn't hold up to close inspection—dark stubble failing to disguise a weak chin, small eyes set too close together, and a thin-lipped leer masquerading as a smile. He'd always been an asshole and apparently hadn't changed with the passing years. The kind of guy who took a tiny bit of power and inflated it into something he used to hammer everyone around him.

I peered at him. "Are you for real? Is there a line outside I missed somehow?"

Sam put his hand on my knee, squeezed gently. "She'll have a beer," he said. When the bartender turned his back on us, Sam rolled his eyes. "Matt takes his job serious."

"Does he own this place now?"

Sam shook his head. "No, Jimmy Ray's got this place."

My heart thumped hard in my chest, and I took a sip of the beer Matt had placed in front of me. The foam tickled my lip, and I almost coughed at the bitter sting of it. I hadn't had a drink since Junie was born, not a single sip. It was on my unwritten list of rules. Turned out I'd lost the taste for it over the years and I pushed the bottle away.

"What are you doing here?" Sam asked. "Seems like an odd choice. You know . . . with everything."

I shrugged. "I needed to talk to Jimmy Ray about something. Heard this might be a good place to catch him."

Sam gave me a sideways glance. "You may not be his favorite person right now."

"What?" I said, startled. "Why?" I couldn't imagine why I was even on Jimmy Ray's radar anymore. We'd given each other a wide berth in the years since we'd split, the occasional mocking wink from across the grocery store parking lot as close as he'd come to acknowledging my existence.

Sam opened his mouth to answer, but one of the strippers sidled up behind him, slung a skinny arm around his neck. "Hey, baby," she said. "Buy me a drink?" She pressed her body into Sam's back, and his face heated red again. Maybe that was why he had a beard, an attempt to hide his tendency to blush, a reaction that probably earned him plenty of shit from Jimmy Ray's crowd.

"I'm in the middle of something," he said, shrugging her off.

She pouted at him, even though she was a couple of decades past the stage where pouting was even moderately endearing. "Awww . . . come on," she said. "One drink." She glanced at me and smiled with blank eyes. I couldn't bring myself to smile back, my gaze falling to the ring of bruises around the crook of her elbow, the scabby track marks on her skin.

"Hey, Maggie," Matt said, rapped twice on the bar with his knuckles to get her attention. "No one's interested in buying you a drink." He paused, smirked. "Or sampling your dried-up old cunt."

"Now, come on," Sam said, but quiet, like he knew better than to contradict Matt. Had learned that lesson the hard way.

Maggie squared her jaw, pushed back her shoulders. But I could see her hands shaking where they rested on her hips. "You can't talk to me like that," she said. "I'm gonna tell Jimmy Ray. That's sexual harassment. You can't do that no more."

Matt laughed. "Oh, shit." He pretended to wipe tears of mirth from his eyes. "Are you serious? You gonna run out and get *Me Too* tattooed on those saggy tits? Goddamn, Maggie, you crack me up." He flapped his bar rag at her. "Get the fuck out of here."

Maggie glanced at me, something timeless and weary passing between us. The world might be changing in some places, but not here. Here it was still the same old merry-go-round of drugs and poverty and women being chewed up and spit out by men. People in other worlds could wear black evening gowns and give speeches about equality and not backing down, but out here in the trenches, we fought our war alone and we lost the battles every day.

I watched as Maggie shuffled off, limping a little in her cheap stilettos. If not for Cal, that could have been my fate, and I had a sudden urge to hug my brother, thank him for the hovering that usually drove me nuts.

"What the fuck are you doing here?" a voice said from behind me. I heard anger in the words, but curiosity, maybe even amusement, in the tone. A shiver worked its way up my spine. Jimmy Ray.

I turned on my bar stool and came face-to-face with my biggest mistake. A lot of people would have fingered Junie for that honor. Getting knocked up the summer before your senior year in high school wasn't exactly genius-level thinking. But I'd never considered Junie a mistake, not even when I had no idea how I was going to afford her or where my next meal was coming from. Because, let's face it, my future wasn't exactly gold-plated before she started growing in my belly. So having her didn't change much, other than the fact that I had an extra mouth to feed. It wasn't like I was giving up college scholarships or trips to distant lands by having a daughter at eighteen. I'd never given much thought to what came after high school, had spent most of my time and energy just trying to survive my childhood. And truth was, Junie had saved me from the inevitable slide into my mother's type of life. I hadn't cared about myself enough to try and be different. But from the moment she was born, I'd cared about Junie. Loved her enough to slam on the brakes and do a one-eighty.

I'd been almost perfect. No drinking, no drugs, no smoking, no stealing or getting in fights. No arrests. No men. Or almost no men. But when I'd screwed up, just the once, I'd screwed up big. Jimmy Ray was never a plan I'd had. I'd like to say he charmed me or that I was lonely, but that wouldn't be the truth. Jimmy Ray was never big on charm. And other than Cal, I'd been a loner all my life. Loneliness was more a permanent state than something I'd ever thought about escaping. It would probably be most accurate to say Jimmy Ray was like an itch I had to scratch. I'd been walking the straight and narrow for almost three years, since the day I'd found out I was pregnant with Junie, and I was starting to chafe under my own restrictions.

Being a good mother hadn't been as effortless as I'd tried to make it seem. There were plenty of days when Junie was little, crying all night with colic as a baby, or whining for a toy I couldn't afford as a toddler, when I'd had to lock myself in the bathroom and scream into a towel. Knot my hands into white-knuckled fists and count to a hundred just to keep from slapping her. Those early years were the worst, when slipping into my mama's brand of motherhood had seemed dangerously close. A hair trigger waiting to be pulled. And then I ran into Jimmy Ray one day at the gas station, and thought maybe he was a way for me to let the pressure off, get a taste of relief.

I'd seen Jimmy Ray around when I was growing up, older than Cal but younger than my mother. I'd known what he was because I wasn't blind. But I'd still fallen for the dark hair and green eyes, the lopsided grin, the tiger tattoo curled around his neck. The scent of danger he wore like cologne. When I was with him, I felt like the old Eve, the one who had flirted with disaster and never cared about how much something might hurt. I hadn't believed him when he said what we had was different, that with me he was a changed man. I knew he was full of shit because I'd listened to a dozen men spout the same lies to my mama over the years, but I'd thought I could contain the damage when we inevitably blew apart. Somehow it had still caught me by surprise, the moment when he'd backhanded me across my own kitchen table, split open my cheek in front of my daughter and kept right on eating his chicken potpie while my blood dripped out from between my shaking fingers. So yeah, I wasn't blind, but I was stupid. I'd thought that I could dip a single toe into the pool. Didn't realize I was drowning until I was completely submerged.

"I'm looking for you," I told him, gripping the seat of my bar stool with both hands to steady myself. He looked older and harder than I remembered, skin starting to loosen at his jaw, deeper lines fanning out from his eyes, one of which was swollen shut, the lid bruised almost black. "What happened?" I asked him. Hoped whoever delivered that punch enjoyed it because it was probably the last thing they ever did on this earth.

Jimmy Ray snorted, took a hit off the beer bottle dangling from his fingers, and then pointed at his eye. "This? Courtesy of your brother. Came in here all fired up a few nights ago. I let him have his shot, because he's a cop and who needs the aggravation." On anyone else it would have smacked of face-saving bravado. On Jimmy Ray, I knew it was the truth. Cal's badge was the only thing that had spared him from a bullet in the head. And now I knew why Sam had worried Jimmy Ray might not want to see me.

"Cal?" I said. "Why?" But I remembered Land's questions about Jimmy Ray the day Junie died. That would have been all Cal needed. He stayed within the letter of the law most of the time now that he was tasked with enforcing it, but he'd learned at my mama's knee. No one messed with Cal's family. We protected each other with bared teeth and claws. No excuses and no forgiveness. And no amount of civilizing, no years of carrying a badge, could ever completely tame that impulse.

Jimmy Ray slammed his beer bottle onto the bar top. "He wanted to see if I was eager to start talking."

"Were you?" I asked, although I already knew the answer. It would take more than a couple of punches for Jimmy Ray to spill his guts if keeping silent was in his best interest.

Jimmy Ray smirked at me. "What do you think?"

I slid off my bar stool and moved closer to him. He threw a look over the bar at Matt, a laugh working its way onto his lips. He always did think women fighting back was funny. He'd usually let you get a few swats in, like a kitten squaring off against a pit bull, before he squashed you. But when I reached out and poked him in the chest, he grabbed my fingers, the smile wiped off his face in an instant. He didn't bend my fingers backward, not yet. But I felt the threat hovering there, tendons poised to snap. "Watch yourself, girl," he said under his breath.

"Do you know anything about it?" I said. "About what happened to Junie?"

He released my hand and gave me a shove backward. "I don't hurt kids," he said. His mouth twisted up, offended. "Jesus."

"I think you'd hurt your own mother, Jimmy Ray, if you stood to gain something by doing it."

Jimmy Ray snorted out a laugh. "Shit, I'd kill that worthless bitch for free. But that's beside the point. There ain't nothin' a couple of twelve-year-old girls could do to or for me that would make killing 'em worth my while."

"Look me in the eye," I said. "Look me in the eye and swear you didn't have anything to do with it."

"Fuck you," he said. "I knew that girl when she was in diapers. You really think I could have killed her that way?"

I knew I shouldn't believe him. But the thing was, I did. Because Jimmy Ray, for all his casual violence, had a set of rules he lived by, just like everyone else. And killing two twelve-year-old girls violated those rules. He could live with beating his girlfriends until they bled, with hooking kids on meth and heroin, with gunning down his competition and leaving them in the woods to rot. But killing two kids in the park? He'd have a hard time looking in the mirror after that. Because, at the end of the day, Jimmy Ray still thought of himself as one of the good guys.

"Enough of this," he said, took a step closer to me. "That the only reason you came here? To accuse me of some bullshit? Or you got something else in mind?" He pushed even closer, the heat of his body leaching into mine. "Because you're looking good, Evie. Real good." He ran his hand down my arm, and God help me, my stomach still flipped. Even after everything. For a moment, I considered taking him up on it. Junie was gone. What did it matter? I could let Jimmy Ray beat me all day and fuck me all night and no one would get hurt but me. If I was aiming for self-destruction, Jimmy Ray was the fastest, most obvious choice. But I still owed Junie some justice, and a detour with Jimmy Ray wouldn't get me where I needed to go. The moment passed, and I took a step backward.

"You don't know anything about it?" I pressed and saw the way Jimmy Ray's fist folded into a knot. I didn't think he'd hit me here, in front of everyone, not least of all because he preferred hitting women who were attached to him. That way he could watch the painful aftermath, make us beg for his forgiveness and ask for a second chance. It wasn't nearly as satisfying to punch someone who could turn and walk away. But I steeled myself anyway, readied myself for a blow. Welcomed it almost.

Jimmy Ray shook his head, spoke through a clenched jaw. "All I know is I didn't do it," he said. Which, when I thought about it later, didn't really answer my question at all.

SEVEN

The smell of stale smoke woke me in the morning, and it took me a few bleary-eyed seconds to realize the stench was from my own hair. I could imagine the way those strippers smelled after a night in the club, although smoke might be the least offensive scent they had to deal with. I rolled over with a groan, squinting against the sunlight that pierced through my curtains and jabbed into my eyes. I hadn't had more than that single sip of beer last night, but my whole body throbbed like I was nursing the world's worst hangover. Even my skin ached. Maybe it was grief, oozing out through my pores. My body had suffered when Junie came into the world. It seemed only fitting that it suffered when she left.

I forced myself out of bed, whimpering a little when my feet hit the floor and I shoved myself to standing. I shuffled to the bathroom and was just heading to the kitchen to put on a pot of coffee when my gaze landed on the patterned curtain blocking off the small dining alcove. It was the one spot I'd avoided looking since the night Cal brought me home from the funeral home. Junie's "room," such as it was. When Junie had been alive, I hadn't thought much about the space. But now that she was gone, it taunted me. Not only because I associated it so strongly with my daughter, but because it was a reminder of another way I'd failed her. What child wants to grow up without a room of her own? Wants to make do with a sectioned-off portion of the living room? Even I'd had a room in the trailer growing up. I had to share it with Cal, and it was hot in the summer and cold in the winter and smelled like mildew and urine. But it was still a room. Four walls and a door. More than Junie ever had. She'd shared a room with me until she was eight and then moved into the alcove. I'd mentioned it to her sometimes, said I was sorry I couldn't give her more, and she'd always scoffed, said she liked her space fine. It had always seemed like she meant it. But now, without her voice competing with the scolding one in my head, I found her assurances hard to believe. If she hadn't been ashamed, then why had she so rarely invited Izzy to our apartment? And even then, only for a quick dinner or to watch a movie, never to spend the night. She always wanted to go to Izzy's, never the other way around. That's another thing no one tells you about dealing with death, how afterward the only voice you can hear is your own, reminding you of everything you did wrong.

I sidled over to the drawn curtain, slowly, like it was a rattler that might bite. Laid my hand gingerly on the cotton fabric. Yellow-and-white paisley. Pottery Barn. I'd done that one thing right, at least. Worked extra shifts at the diner until I could afford to let Junie pick something nice, quality, not some shiny, polyester crap from the clearance bin. It seemed a silly distinction now, but it had mattered to me at the time.

I drew the curtain back, the hooks tinkling against the wooden rod Cal had installed one snowy December night. It had been her Christmas present that year, a can of sunny yellow paint for the alcove walls, new bedding, the curtain. A small bookcase I'd rescued from the thrift store and painted white. A pink glass bedside lamp Cal's contribution.

The room had changed very little in the ensuing years. The books on the bookcase morphing from children's to young adult. A small dresser squeezed in against the far wall, the top littered with earrings and spare change and accumulated junk. But the tiny twin bed still had the same quilt, the pink lamp still perched on her bedside table.

I took a step beyond the curtain, and the smell of Junie smacked me in the face. The scent I'd been searching for when I'd kissed her in the morgue. Her hair, her skin, the mint gum she always chewed, the grapefruit bodywash she loved. A small, choked sound escaped me, and I covered my mouth with one hand, trying to hold it in. The sudden surge of pain was so huge, so monumental, that I feared expelling it would rip my insides out, lungs and heart and stomach gushing out of me, a bloody pile of organs left on the floor. But my hand was no match for my grief, and the bed rose up to greet me as I fell, burying my face in her pillow to muffle my screams.

I don't know how long I thrashed on her bed, slamming my face into the mattress and scratching at my own skin. Trying to get away from the anguish that had burrowed into the marrow of my bones. *Go ahead and give it your best shot,* the pain said. *I'll be here waiting when you give up.* And eventually, I did. My sobs winding down like a toy with a dying battery, my body limp and spent, hair sweat-plastered to my skull. The pain was still there, just as it had promised. But I could carry it now. For a little while, at least. And that was something.

I rolled over, stared through tear-swollen lids at the constellation stickers plastered to Junie's ceiling. Probably every second kid in America had a set, but we'd both been enthralled by them, as if they were rare gems instead of a random Dollar General find. Spent long minutes lying here side by side at night, heads touching on her pillow, watching the planets glow.

"Hey, Junie," I said. "Are you up there?" I hoped she was. Hoped my girl was flying, somewhere beyond the stars.

The day stretched out before me, empty and pointless. I could go to the diner, but I knew Thomas would march my ass straight back out again. I had to wait a few more days before I could plead my case and beg to go back to work. *You find him,* my mama's voice hissed inside my head. But I had no idea how. I'd talked to Jimmy Ray and gotten exactly nowhere. And I'd only thought of him because Land had mentioned him first. I wasn't a detective. I wasn't even a cop. I was a thirty-year-old with a high school diploma, a dead daughter, and not much else. *Well, then you might as well say, "Fuck it." Let the bastard get away. 'Cause ain't nobody gonna give a shit about who killed Junie except you. Not really.* My mama's voice again. And true words, even though she'd never actually spoken them. Well, not exactly true. Cal cared. Almost as much as I did, I suspected. But he was hampered by his status as a cop. Everyone knew him, same as they did me, but he was on the other side of the law now. He might have been the Cal they fished with as kids or stole beers with as teenagers. But he was Cal the cop now, and that changed things. That was a shift you didn't come back from, not around here. People liked him fine, but they weren't ever going to tell him their secrets.

But people might talk to me, crazy Lynette Taggert's daughter. I was one of them. Had grown up here and still hadn't managed to claw my way up or out. So, yeah, they might talk. If I could figure out who to corner and the right questions to ask. I thought back to that night at the funeral home, the things Land had said. Asking us if the girls had been acting any different lately, if we'd noticed a change. I truly hadn't. But that didn't mean there hadn't been one. Junie and I had been close, closer than most mothers and daughters. But I wasn't stupid in the ways of teenage girls. I'd been one myself not all that long ago, and I knew the secrets they squirreled away, the crazy, self-destructive things they sometimes did in the mistaken belief that they were too young for anything really terrible to actually touch them. Hell, I'd been as wild as they come at Junie's age. Had already smoked my first cigarette and nursed my first hangover by twelve. Had lost my virginity at thirteen to one of my mom's boyfriends. Not rape, exactly. More of a lazy kind of coercion—*come on, baby, you know you want to, I'll make it good*— where it's easier to go along and get it over with than put up a fight. At least then you can lie to yourself after and say it had been partly your own idea. I knew more than I wanted to about the secret lives of teenage girls.

I sat up on Junie's bed, remembering the notebook I'd seen her writing in sometimes. She always said it was for her poetry. Read to me from the wrinkled pages. But whenever I got too close, she hunched over, hugging it to her body, where I couldn't get more than a glimpse of the words written there. At the time, I'd pictured hastily scrawled notes about boys she thought were cute. Maybe even harsh words aimed at me on the rare occasions when we fought, usually about something stupid like her wearing her coat to school or not staying up too late on school nights. But what if there was something more? Part of me didn't want to look for fear I would find another way to punish myself after the fact. But I couldn't let it go, either.

The cops had already given her room a perfunctory search, but hadn't found anything as far as I knew. They were looking for some big smoking gun that I could have told them wasn't there before they ever set foot inside. I was on the hunt for something less obvious. I let my eyes wander around the room, the small space bereft of many hiding places. A quick rummage through her dresser drawers yielded nothing more exciting than a pack of gum and a few loose marbles from a set Cal had given her years ago. I thought back to my own childhood, the places I stashed money or secrets in hopes my mama wouldn't find either. I slid my hand between Junie's mattress and box spring and hit pay dirt, pulling out the notebook with *Property of Junie* scrawled in gold marker across the navy blue cover.

I pulled back the cover carefully, almost wincing against what I might find. Junie's presence enveloped me as I read her words, saw the doodles she'd drawn on the edges of the pages. I hoped she didn't mind, my snooping into her private world. I took my time, running my fingers over places where her pen had dug into the paper, smiling at quick notes she'd jotted complaining about a school assignment or lamenting my inability to cook. *Had a fight w/ Izzy, but we're good now*, adorned the top of one page, followed by a heart. There was no mention of boys or drugs or sneaking out. Nothing that set my alarm bells ringing. Nothing until the final pages. Where in a bottom corner, writing cramped like she was fighting to get the words out, Junie wrote: *Worried about Izzy. I told her he's too old. But she's not listening. To anyone. She says it's love, but it's really only lust. Gross. Just thinking about it makes me sick. I wish she would wake up.* She'd written the word *up* with such force that her pen had torn through the paper.

My breath gusted out of me. Here was something I could grab onto. A place to start, at least. Which was more than I'd had an hour ago. The day opened up in front of me. A reason to stand up and move. A reason to keep going.

EIGHT

Martin Luther King Jr. Middle School was twelve miles outside of town, down a winding road off the highway that hid it from view. It served the kids of the entire spread-out county, some riding the bus more than an hour each way to sit in an old, drafty building without enough teachers or anywhere near enough funds. They'd renamed the school a few years ago in a nod to diversity. When I'd attended, the county had been virtually all white. But nowadays, with the chicken-processing plant perched on the edge of the county line, the kids of immigrants roamed the halls, their parents taking jobs no locals would touch, even when other steady employment was almost impossible to come by. I'd listened to plenty of bitching about the name change while serving coffee in the diner, endless complaints about political correctness or, as one old-timer put it, "this bullshit idea that everybody's got to be equal." People around here didn't like being force-fed progress, even when it could be argued that a mouthful was long overdue. I somehow doubted the name change did much to alter the reality for those kids, who were always going to be outsiders. Junie had hated the place, couldn't wait to start high school in another year. I hadn't had the heart to tell her that Harry S. Truman High School wasn't much better, maybe even worse. Too many kids without a lot of hope for the future crowded into an even smaller space. From my graduating class, only a handful of kids had gone on to college. And of those, the majority had come back to Barren Springs without a degree. It's hard to move up in the world when you've never seen it done.

I counted myself lucky that I'd graduated at all. Seventh grade was the first time I'd set foot in an actual school. Cal and I were "educated" in the holler. My mama taught us our ABCs and not much else. Our closest neighbor, Miss Eileen, taught us to read and to do basic math in exchange for cigarettes from Mama. Seventh grade was the first time I'd realized that there was poor and then there was *poor*. And we were the second kind. Most people around here aren't exactly rolling in dough, but there's a difference between the people who live closer to town and the ones who stay hidden in the hollers. We were the ones who learned to read from the meth addict down the road, if we learned at all; the ones who wore not just hand-me-downs but clothes that didn't fit or came covered in stains of unknown origin. We had a hungry, feral look about us, even on the rare times our bellies were full, which made us instantly recognizable targets. Or it would have if our mama's reputation hadn't preceded us. Our status as the poorest of poor white trash trumped only by our mama's penchant for casual violence. Everybody remembered the kid who'd thrown a rock at Cal down by the river one day. No one could say if he'd actually meant to hit Cal or it had been an unlucky throw. Hadn't mattered to our mama, though. Next time we'd seen that kid, he'd been sporting a busted-up hand and scared, skittish eyes. Never would come within a country mile of either one of us again.

Usually Junie rode the bus home from school, often going home with Izzy on days I worked past dinnertime. On the few occasions I picked her up from school, it had always been controlled chaos when the bell rang, and today was no exception. Kids spilled out of the doors like marbles shot from a cannon as I slid into a parking spot. I noticed a few security guards near the buses, and I wondered if they were a new addition or if I never had a reason to notice them before. Either way, I guessed they wouldn't look too kindly on an adult approaching the kids, even if I did appear relatively harmless. Which meant I needed to intercept Hallie before they noticed me.

Junie and Izzy had been an almost closed loop of friendship. A fact that always made me nervous. I told myself my anxiousness stemmed from worrying about what might happen if the friendship blew up and Junie was left adrift and alone. Or wanting her to have more friends so she wasn't isolated. Growing up, Cal had been my only anchor, and now, as an adult, I still had trouble broadening my circle. Felt unmoored without Cal close by. I didn't want that for Junie. Those reasons were both true. But they weren't the truest one. Still, Junie and Izzy's friendship wasn't completely impenetrable. There were a few girls who hovered on the outside edges, who received birthday party invites or sat with Junie and Izzy at lunch. The one I knew best, Hallie Marshall, had been to the apartment a few times, had shown up in social media pictures next to Junie and Izzy.

I stood near my car, eyes scanning the doors of the school until

I saw Hallie walk out, her reddish hair covered by a gray beanie. When I called her name, she pivoted, brought one hand up to block the sun as she peered at me.

"Hi, Hallie," I said as I approached. "I'm Junie's mom. We've met a few times."

"I remember," she said, voice cautious. She clutched a notebook to her chest like a shield. Around her, kids peeled off toward the buses, eyeing us with curiosity but not slowing down.

"Can I talk to you?" I asked.

Hallie glanced at the buses and then nodded. "For a second. I don't want to miss my bus."

"Okay, sure." I stepped away from the doors and Hallie trailed behind me. When I turned around, she was biting her bottom lip, her eyes on the ground.

"I'm really sorry about Junie," she whispered. "And Izzy, too."

I knew people were trying to be kind, but I was already tired of this ritual. Did people actually think their being sorry helped? That my hearing an endless litany of worthless words over and over and over again made anything better? But Hallie was just a kid, I reminded myself, the same age as Junie. I swallowed down what I really wanted to say and managed a thank-you instead.

"That's what I wanted to talk to you about," I said. "Was Izzy dating an older guy?"

Hallie's eyes flew up to mine, and I knew right then she hadn't been raised in a house like the one where I grew up. She had no poker face. My mother would have eaten her alive. "What?" she managed to stumble out, her cheeks flaring red. "No. I don't know."

I raised my eyebrows at her and waited. I figured it would take twenty seconds of silence to break her, but it only took ten. "I mean, she wasn't like *dating* him. But she liked him." Hallie paused, shifting her weight from foot to foot. "They messed around some."

"Who was he?" I asked, my heart a steady drumbeat pounding *got him got him got him.*

Hallie shrugged. "I don't know. Honest," she added when she glanced at my face. "Izzy would never say."

"Did Junie know who it was?"

"Yeah, I think so. But she always kept Izzy's secrets." Hallie took a step closer to me, lowered her voice. "They fought about it, though. Junie was threatening to tell someone if Izzy didn't stop. She seemed really worried about Izzy."

"Do you know how old this guy was?" I asked. *Eighteen*, I was thinking. *Please say eighteen and not something worse.*

"*Old*," Hallie said. "I don't know exactly. But maybe thirty?"

"Why would you say that?" I tried to keep my voice steady even as my stomach bottomed out.

"Just the way they talked about him. He wasn't a teenager. Not even close." Hallie looked over her shoulder, started shuffling backward. "I gotta go. I'm gonna miss the bus." When she met my eyes again, I could see it there, something she wanted to say but wasn't going to. Something that was trapped behind her clenched teeth.

"Hallie, wait." I reached forward and snagged at the sleeve of her sweatshirt, but she pivoted away from me.

"I can't. I have to go."

I watched her walk away, her eyes on the sidewalk. Frustration pounded through me, and I could feel the part of me that belonged to my mama wanting to race after her and grab a handful of her red hair in my fist. Jerk her bald-headed until she talked. Someone yelled to her from the bus, and she picked up her pace, grabbing the handrail on the bus steps to swing herself inside. Just before she disappeared, she looked back at me. "Talk to your brother," she called, barely loud enough for me to catch the words. By the time the syllables had sorted themselves out inside my head, the door was closing. As the bus pulled away, I caught of glimpse of Hallie's face in the window, her eyes skating away from mine.

Cal. Who loved Junie like his own. Who'd grown up breaking the law—stealing food when I was hungry, fighting kids who wronged me, running drug errands for Mama so I didn't have to—and now lived to follow it. Cal, who all the women wanted but could never seem to catch. He always said it was because he was focused on work or they were too needy, wanted too much of him—a shudder ran through me—but maybe they were just too old.

NINE

Thomas almost bowled me over with a stinking bag of trash when he barreled out through the back door of the diner. "Jesus Christ," he said, pivoting to avoid me at the last second, the plastic bag thunking against my hip. "What the hell are you doing out here, Eve?"

I leaned sideways, wrinkling my nose at the smell. "Sorry. Didn't mean to trip you."

Thomas heaved the sack over the railing and into the open dumpster, the lid closing again with a hollow clank. He wiped his hands on his apron. "Didn't answer my question," he said.

I shrugged. "Having a smoke." Truth was, after talking to Hallie, I hadn't known what to do with myself. I'd called Cal, but he hadn't answered. I couldn't stand the thought of going back to my empty apartment. The diner was the closest thing I had to a home. And if that thought wasn't depressing enough, sitting out here with the smell of rotted trash in the air and broken bottles and cigarette butts at my feet really sealed the deal.

Thomas lowered himself next to me, wincing a little. He was getting too old to be on his feet all day, bent over that cooktop. But I knew he'd never give it up. Would work that kitchen until the day he keeled over on the cracked linoleum floor. "Since when do you smoke?"

"Since my kid got murdered."

That would have shut most people up. But not Thomas, who never was shy with his opinion. "Nasty habit," he said with a shake of his head. I felt him look at me, his dark eyes running over the side of my face. "How you doing, sweet girl?" he asked finally.

Tears pricked my eyes, but I blinked them back. I hadn't seen Thomas or Louise since Izzy's funeral, where I'd spotted them across the church and just as quickly avoided all eye contact. I could hold myself together around most people. People who didn't really care about me or Junie. People who barely knew us or made mouth noises about how sorry they were. But Thomas and Louise had known Junie since the day she was born. Thomas had rocked Junie for hours when she had colic as a baby. Louise had been the one to teach me to talk to Junie even when she was too young to know what I was saying. My mama thought words were wasted on babies: *What're you talking to her for? Only thing she understands is your tit in her mouth.* Without Thomas and Louise those early years would have been so much harder. They had held Junie in their arms and watched her grow. Loved teasing me about how smitten I was with my daughter. They knew the truth. Outside I was still a functioning human. But inside I was ripped to shreds. "Not so good," I told him, flicked the cigarette away. I didn't even know why I was smoking it.

It *was* a nasty habit, made my mouth taste like my mama used to smell. Sour and edged with violence. It scared me a little how comforting that taste was right now. "I want to come back to work."

Thomas mulled that over. I could see his brain working behind his eyes. "You sure that's a good idea? I can float you a loan, you know. No need for you to do more than you're able right now."

I shook my head. "I can't sit around all day. It's making me crazy." *Making me think about doing things, things only my mama would approve of.* I picked up a pebble and bounced it in my hand. "I promise I'll behave. I won't cry into anyone's coffee, if that's what you're worried about."

Thomas made a gruff sound in his throat. "I don't care if you sob all day long. It's not you I'm worried about. It's all the lookie-loos around here. Asking questions and sticking their noses in where they don't belong."

"I can handle it," I said, but my words had the ring of bravado rather than truth. Thomas patted my knee lightly. "Why don't you wait and see," he said. "Give it a few more days."

We sat in silence then, listening to stray bits of trash blowing up against the chain-link fence across the alley. In the distance I could hear occasional cars passing on the highway, the smell of the dumpster thankfully overpowered by the wind bringing a faint scent of spring flowers. It was surprisingly peaceful back here. I felt hidden, and part of me never wanted to get up, had a vague notion of roosting on these steps for the foreseeable future.

"Oh Lord," Thomas said. "We got company." He stood up, dusting off the seat of his pants. "And not the good kind."

A police cruiser was easing down the alley toward us, tires crunching over old gravel. From the outline of the driver, I knew it wasn't Cal. Too bulky, not tall enough, and my stomach took a steep dive even as I told myself to stop it. Nothing to be scared of. I was a victim's mother now, someone to be handled with kid gloves.

The cruiser pulled up alongside us, and the driver's window went down with a whir. "Hey there, Thomas," Land said, eyes hidden behind reflective sunglasses.

Thomas didn't respond other than a faint nod. Land's job might have been to protect and serve, but those duties always came with a little dose of attitude when the person Land was protecting and serving had some extra pigment to their skin. Like he wasn't doing his job, he was doing them a favor. And they'd owe him eventually. The half smile slid off Land's face as he turned to look at me. "Eve," he said. "We need to talk."

"Okay," I said without moving.

"In private," Land clarified.

"Why don't you two come on inside," Thomas said. "Have a cup of coffee while you chat."

Land's gaze slid back to Thomas, or I assumed it did because his head turned that direction. "Nah, we're fine out here." He gestured to me with one hand extended out his window. "Come on, Eve. I ain't got all day."

I stood up, legs heavy, and started down the steps. Thomas's hand shot out and caught at my forearm, bringing me up short. "You need me," he said low, "I'm right inside."

I nodded. It occurred to me for the first time that maybe I wasn't the only one in this town with bad memories of Land, whose steps slowed every time he slid into view. I stood by Land's passenger door until Thomas went back inside, had to take a quick step backward when Land shoved open the door and motioned for me to hop in with an impatient hand.

I settled into the passenger seat carefully, my body folded into itself. I hadn't been inside Land's car in years, and I'd sworn I never would be again. "You got any idea why I'm here?" Land asked.

"No." Although I was pretty sure I did.

Land sighed. "I got a call from Hallie Marshall's mama. Said you were harassing her girl outside of school today."

I turned toward him. "I was not harassing her. I asked her a couple of questions, that's all."

Land mirrored my position, one beefy hand coming up to clutch the top of the steering wheel, sunlight glinting off the wedding ring he still wore, although his wife, Mabel, had died two years ago. Probably sick of looking at his smug face every day. Even across the car, I could smell stale coffee on his breath. "Since when is it your job to go around asking questions? You got a police badge I don't know about? You need to let us do what we're trained to do, Eve."

"Okay, then," I said, heat rising in my chest. "Have *you* talked to Hallie?" Land shook his head, and before he could say anything more, I plowed on, "Well, you should have. Did you know Izzy was involved with an older guy? A lot older? That could have something to do with the murders. If I waited for you all to fig—"

"We already know that," Land said.

All the air went out of my tirade, my mouth left hanging open in the middle of a word. "Know what?"

"About the older guy. Cal heard it from Junie."

It should have relieved me, Hallie's words about Cal making sense now. She wasn't pointing me toward Izzy's older man, but toward someone who might know more about him. But I couldn't wrap my head around it, the fact that Cal had known about Izzy and hadn't told me. And I hated that Land was a step ahead of me. Always. "Who was it?" I demanded.

Land shook his head. "We're still figuring that out. But I wouldn't tell you even if I knew for sure. You don't have any business getting involved in this."

"She was my daughter," I burst out. "How can you say it's not my business?"

"I heard you went and confronted Jimmy Ray, too," Land said, like I hadn't even spoken. "That's a bad idea, Eve. Don't need to remind you how that turned out for you last time, do I?" His eyes flicked toward my wrist, his hand following the movement, and I snatched my arm away.

"Don't touch me!"

Land pulled back, a smirk chasing its way across his face. "Jesus, calm down," he said. "Every time you see me you're like a cat on a hot tin roof." He lowered his voice even though there was no one but me to hear him. "It was only a blow job. Can't believe it's still got you worked up after all this time. Know for a fact it wasn't the first one you'd ever given."

My throat burned at his words; my never-healed-quite-right wrist bones ached under my skin. My stomach heaved as if it were all happening right now instead of on a rainy October night almost a decade ago. It had been the end for Jimmy Ray and me for a while. We'd both known it, me because I wasn't going to let him keep on hitting me in front of my daughter and him because it had reached the point where the fun of smacking me around was outweighed by what a pain in the ass I'd turned into. Calling the cops. Not fighting back, exactly, but resisting him just the same, no matter what he threatened. But with Jimmy Ray everything had to be on his terms. Even the leaving. And he wasn't quite ready yet. Even after he'd split my lip and blackened my eyes, snapped my wrist bones between his hands, he hadn't been ready to let go. Had told me he'd see me soon, winked as they'd loaded him into the back of the police cruiser, the spinning lights making the world tilt and whirl in front of me.

Land had taken me to the hospital because Cal was watching over Junie, tucking her back into bed and telling her lies about what had happened to her mama. Land had stayed with me until they'd wrapped my arm and told me to come back in two days for a permanent cast. And then he'd led me back out to his cruiser, parked on the dark edge of the hospital parking lot, and told me the drill.

"You're causing me a lot of trouble," he'd said. "This business with you and Jimmy Ray."

"Me?" The word coming out smushed and garbled between my swollen lips. "I just want him to go away. We're over. I don't understand why you can't make him leave me alone. Isn't that your job?" I wasn't worried about myself. What was one more beating in the scheme of things? But Junie, every day she was growing older, cataloguing more of the world around her, remembering. And I wasn't sure how much longer I could keep Cal contained, promising him I could handle it, swearing I'd never speak to him again if he put himself in the middle, risked his job over an idiot like Jimmy Ray. Secretly, I worried he'd try something and end up dead. Cal was smart and strong, but Jimmy Ray didn't care about anything except his own survival, and that made him the more dangerous man.

Land had sighed, his default expression of choice, and turned toward me. Both his mustache and his belly were smaller then, but he still had the outlines of the same man. One who'd worn his authority for so long, and with so little resistance, that he took it all for granted. "Well, that's the thing," he said. "I can't do my job, not the way I'm supposed to, when you've got me at odds with Jimmy Ray." He spread his hands in the darkness. "He and I, we do for each other. You understand?"

I'd heard rumors about the arrangement between Jimmy Ray and Land. Hell, everyone had. That they scratched each other's backs. That whatever they had worked out was the reason Jimmy Ray might get arrested for beating a girlfriend or drunk driving, but never for anything more serious. And never for anything that wouldn't quietly go away the next morning.

"No," I said. "I don't understand. Are you not going to help me, then?"

"Look," Land said, his voice slow, like he was talking to a child. "I know what Jimmy Ray does. But he keeps it away from this town. He keeps his people in line. No drug murders. No dead bodies filling up my streets."

I snorted. "Yeah, because he dumps them in the woods instead for the wild hogs to eat."

"I don't care what the fuck he does with them, long as they don't show up on my watch. No one gives a shit about what happens to those people, anyway. Ones that are all mixed up in Jimmy Ray's world. Good riddance, far as I'm concerned." One of Land's hands inched closer to my leg, not quite touching. I watched it the way you would a spider skittering toward you. Knowing it was coming, but hoping for a detour at the last second. "That's the deal we got. He keeps his business under control, and I look the other way. Neither one of us wants a war. It's better this way."

"Better for who?" I asked, shifting my body away from that creeping hand.

"For everyone," Land snapped. "That's what I'm trying to tell you." The rain had picked up, sharp taps on the roof and a steady stream across the windshield, closing us in. "And now you're wanting me to disrupt all that." Land shook his head. "It's a problem, Eve. It's gonna cause me some grief."

My stomach sank. I knew what he meant. A little tit for tat. How many times had I seen my mama caught in the same trap? It seemed the fate of women the world over. "What do you want?" I said, voice flat. I'd heard whispers about Land for years, so I already knew. But I was going to make him say it, at least.

Land eyed me for a second and then took my hand, limp and cold, in his and pressed it against the front of his pants. Rubbed my slack palm over his hardening dick. "But with your mouth."

I swallowed, kept my eyes on the rain pelting the windshield. "And if I do?"

"Then I take care of Jimmy Ray for you. Make sure he stays gone." He pushed up into my hand, his breath coming faster.

I wanted my hand to come alive, pictured my numb fingers closing hard, nails digging into flesh. Leaving blood and permanent damage behind. But Junie is what stopped me. The vision of her face, eyes wide and cheeks streaked with tears. Her tiny voice— *Mama?*—as she watched Jimmy Ray crush my wrist in his fist and heard me scream out in pain. I hadn't been able to protect her from that. But this could be a secret. She would never have to know, never have to see with her own eyes what I'd been reduced to. We'd be free of Jimmy Ray, once and for all. And I'd be the mother she needed from now on, the mother she deserved. No more mistakes. It seemed almost like poetic justice, in a way. Jimmy Ray was my fault, my moment of weakness. This would be my punishment.

It didn't take Land long, I'll give him that. Thank God for small mercies, as my mama would say. But he was rough, hand knotted in my hair, pushing down while his hips shoved up, barely giving me room to breathe. Rough enough that my injured mouth started bleeding again, red smeared across his skin by the time I was done.

In the end, it was worth it. Land was as good as his word, and

Jimmy Ray stayed away. Cal kept his job and his life. And Junie was spared watching her mother being beat to hell over and over again. If she remembered Jimmy Ray and what he'd done to me, she never mentioned it. Maybe she'd forgotten, or maybe it was locked inside her mind. One of those hazy early-childhood memories that could be chalked up to a bad dream or an overactive imagination. But I never forgot. Not Jimmy Ray and especially not Land. My wrist still throbbed on occasion, when I slept on it funny or saw Jimmy Ray's truck in town. But the memory of Land—a swirl of bitterness and shame in the back of my throat—that taste never went away.

TEN

I don't know if it was a product of our chaotic upbringing—never knowing when our next meal might appear, constantly bombarded with strange faces—but Cal and I had both grown into creature-of-habit adults. Neither one of us liked surprises, not even the good ones. We weren't fans of new places or changes in routine, constantly trying to restore order in our lives. If Cal wasn't at work or visiting me at the diner, he could reliably be found in a handful of places: his apartment or mine, the bar next to the sub shop having a beer, the laundromat reading the paper and watching his clothes spin around in circles. I'd tried all of those places and seen no trace of his truck. That left our Mama's trailer, and I wasn't going there again anytime soon, and Cal's secret fishing spot.

He'd been going to the edge of Jackson Creek to fish for as long as I could remember. When we were growing up, his hands smelled like fish guts more often than not. A scent that still made my mouth water and my stomach cramp with excitement because as vile as the smell was, at least it meant I was going to be fed. Cal didn't need to fish to feed his belly anymore, but I knew the ritual relaxed him; the isolation soothed something inside him, some jagged edge that would never quite be rubbed smooth. I understood it because I had the same rough spot inside myself. Junie had helped smother it, but it was emerging in her absence, a sharp, hard weapon in my gut.

Jackson Creek was actually a river and it ran for miles, tucked away in the woods in some spots, out in the wide open in others. It ran deep and fast at one end, slowed to almost a trickle, then opened up into a flat, calm pool good for skinny-dipping before it surged into the woods again. Everyone around these parts had a relationship with the creek, but hardly anyone knew of Cal's spot, or if they did, they lacked the dedication to reach it. You had to hike in, risk ticks and brambles, thorns scratching your arms and catching in your hair. But Cal swore his spot had the best fish around, fat and shimmering in the sun, so close to the surface you could practically pluck them out with your hands.

And sure enough, his truck was parked in the woods where the trail to his fishing spot began. I sighed, pulling my hair back into a ponytail and yanking down the sleeves of my shirt before I followed him in. By the time I arrived—a twenty-minute trek that felt more like an hour—the sun was high in the sky and sweat was making a slow descent down my back. At least it was still only spring, the summer's relentless heat only a whisper on the warming wind.

"Hey," I said, stepping out onto the flat rock where Cal sat perched over the water, fishing rod extended into the creek. I could see three fish already resting in his ice-filled cooler.

"Hey," Cal said without turning around. "I heard you about ten minutes ago. Always know it's you when it sounds like a herd of elephants is tramping through the woods. You would make a crap spy."

"Yeah, well, spy's never been high on my career list." I lowered myself down next to him, shoving my sleeves up and swiping a hand across the back of my sweaty neck. "How long you been out here?"

Cal shrugged. "Not too long." He looked as terrible as I felt, dark smudges under his eyes and his eyelids puffy from recent tears I knew he'd deny shedding. "I needed a day where no one was looking at me, waiting for me to crack, you know?"

"Yeah," I said. "I know."

Cal adjusted his hold on the rod, reeled in the line a little. The sunlight made his hair glow gold, his eyelashes making hazy shadows on his cheeks. "Land told me about Hallie and her mom," he said.

I sighed, tipped my face up to the sun and let it paint patterns on my closed eyelids. It felt like warm thumbs pressing against my skin, and the sensation brought the sting of tears. I opened my eyes and turned my face away. "What? Are you and Land tag-teaming me now?" I asked. "I'm guessing you're playing good cop because God knows Land always plays the bad one."

"What's that supposed to mean?"

"Nothing," I mumbled.

Cal laid a hand on my arm, tugging slightly until I turned and looked at him. "I'm not trying to ambush you or tag-team you or whatever. I was worried when Land told me. You can't go off half-cocked, Evie, confronting everyone who—"

I jerked my arm away from him. "I already got the lecture, but thanks."

"Jesus, would you listen to me for one goddamn second? I'm not going to lecture you. I'm trying to apologize."

That stopped me. "For what?"

Cal ran a hand through his hair. "For not telling you about Izzy. I promised Junie I wouldn't." He raised his hand in my direction when I opened my mouth to speak. "But I would have, eventually. I wanted to figure out exactly what was going on first. And help Junie see that it would be better if you knew. And Izzy's parents, too."

I slumped, all the fight gone out of me. I liked it better when anger was sluicing through my blood. Rage blotted out everything else. "I thought Junie told me everything. Why would she want to keep that a secret from me?"

Cal paused, and I knew he was doing that thing where he weighed how much to say. Cal was always careful that way, wanting to make sure he got the words just right before he released them. He reached over and tapped the ball of my shoulder with one finger. "You have kind of a big chip right here when it comes to the Logans. Junie wasn't blind to it, you know. She probably didn't want to give you any reason to cut off her friendship with Izzy."

Welcome heat blazed up my spine, and I twisted away from him. "What are you talking about? I don't have a chip on my shoulder about the Logans. I don't even *know* them!"

Cal raised his eyebrows at me. "No, but you know the *idea* of them. Nice little ranch house, two cars, married, maybe some money in the bank." I stared at him blankly, and he sighed, leaned forward to rest his elbows on his knees, fishing rod almost touching his forehead. "Come on, Evie, you know what I'm saying. They're the total opposite of how we grew up. Pretty much picture-perfect compared to our disaster."

I crossed my arms and tucked my elbows in. A shield made of limbs. "The total opposite of how Junie grew up, too, is that what you're saying?"

"See?" Cal said. "That's exactly what I'm talking about with the chip. I wasn't even thinking about you and Junie, and your mind automatically goes there, comparing, and always assuming you'd come up short."

"I did come up short," I said. "My daughter is dead."

"Yeah, well," Cal said after a pause, "so is theirs."

I didn't want to have this conversation, to be reminded the Logans had suffered a loss equal to mine. I pointed at Cal's line. "I think you've got something."

He reeled the fish in with practiced ease, slid the hook from its gaping mouth, and set it next to the others in the cooler. I'd grown up killing things, threading wiggling worms onto barbed hooks, slitting open the stomachs of still gasping fish, pulling steaming guts from barely dead deer, twisting a chicken's neck with my bare hands. It had never bothered me before. Animals were food, and food wasn't always easy to come by. Squeamish meant hungry, and there wasn't much worse than hungry. But today I had to turn away from the sight of that fish, its mouth still opening and closing as it lay on top of the ice. Had to put my hands under my thighs to resist the urge to throw it back into the water, to give it one more chance to live.

"I think maybe it was because of the guy," I said as Cal dropped his line back into the water. "The one Izzy was involved with. Maybe that's why they were killed."

Cal gave a noncommittal grunt. "How'd you know about Izzy's guy anyway? If Junie never told you?"

I kept my gaze on the water, watching it flow over rock. Thought about Junie's diary, tucked now into my top dresser drawer. I wasn't going to give it up, let strangers pore over Junie's secret thoughts and feelings. It was one remaining link to my daughter that I didn't have to share. "I didn't really. Just heard a few rumors floating around recently and figured if they were true, Hallie would be the one to know."

I could feel Cal's eyes on me, probably trying to decide if I was telling him the truth. "Let me clean you a fish or two," he said finally. "You've lost weight. You can take this home and fry it up for dinner."

"I have food."

"But you're not eating it." He reached over and laid a hand on my back. "Not eating isn't going to bring her back."

Anger sizzled up my spine, hot and fierce enough that I wondered how it didn't burn his hand right through my skin. "And eating is?"

"No," Cal agreed. "But you still have to do it anyway." He reeled in his line, set his pole down carefully. Growing up, he was the only kid I knew who'd never accidentally hooked someone. He was never careless with other people, only with himself.

"Do you have any idea who the guy is?" I asked. "The one Izzy was messing around with?"

Cal kept his eyes on the fish he was scaling, knife glinting in the sun. "You know I couldn't tell you, even if we did."

"Does that mean yes?" I pressed.

Cal gave me a quick half smile. "It doesn't mean no."

I took a deep breath, one part of my mind screaming at me to shut up, already knowing how dumb and destructive I was being. "When Hallie told me to talk to you, I thought, for a split second that maybe it was you."

"Maybe what was me?" Cal asked, forehead furrowed. He was genuinely confused by my comment, I realized, and I felt like one of those men who confess a long-dead affair in an attempt to ease their own guilty conscience. They might feel better afterward, but the wife never does.

"Never mind," I mumbled, picking up Cal's extra knife and reaching for a fish. "It was stupid."

"Wait." Cal's hand stopped moving, silver scales stuck to his fingers. "You thought *I* was the guy fooling around with Izzy? A twelve-year-old?"

"Not really," I said. "I just . . . You never date anyone, and Hallie said to talk to you . . ." I trailed off, watching shock and anger and a baffled, bruised disappointment skate across Cal's face. It jolted me, that look. Because while I'd seen it on Cal's face a handful of times before, I'd never seen in directed at me.

"I never date anyone because I'm always working!" Cal said. "And who the fuck is there worth dating around here, anyway?" He shook his head, and when he spoke again, his voice was lower, tinged with weariness. "I can't believe you would think that. Even for a second. What have I ever, *ever* done that would make you think something like that about me?"

I opened my mouth to protest, defend myself, but nothing came out. Because the fact was, I *had* thought it, even if only for a split second. My life with Cal unfurled inside me: nights huddled together in one bed, staying warm with gangly limbs tangled around each other; lessons on how to hook a fish or gut a deer; Cal taking the blame for me, whenever and however he could, always trying to spare me pain; his face lighting up the first time Junie said his name. All the times he'd given me the benefit of the doubt, looked the other way, turned the other cheek. I'd thought my love for Cal transcended my mama's horrible lessons. Turned out I simply hadn't been tested. Because Junie's death had brought it all bubbling to the surface. That fundamental instinct to always watch your own back, never trust anyone, never let your guard down. Our family stuck together against outsiders, but that didn't mean we wouldn't turn on each other, quick and deadly as vipers. I'd thought Junie's death had left no room for any other grief, but sadness welled up inside me, pushing against my throat and the backs of my eyes.

"I'm sorry," I managed, finally. It wasn't even close to enough, but what else was there to say?

"Forget it." Cal flapped a hand at me and then split open the fish's belly, slippery guts falling into the water.

I knew we'd never mention it again because that wasn't Cal's way. He wasn't the type to nurse grievances and fling them back at you on some later date. But I knew that this moment would always be there between us like a sharp rock in your shoe, making some steps perfectly normal and others destined to bring a stab of tender pain so that you always have to walk carefully, just in case. The knowledge broke my heart, but I'd had to ask the question. This was bigger than me and Cal. This was about Junie. And I'd hurt myself, and anyone else, a thousand different ways if it meant I could give her some kind of justice.

ELEVEN

No one ever tells you about the time you lose. The well-meaning bring food or send flowers. The worried check you for signs you might hurt yourself and squirrel away the pills and guns. The professionals press slick pamphlets into your hands. Lists of support groups and 800 numbers. Signs that prove your grieving is normal. Lack of appetite. Sleeping too much or not at all. Anger. Depression. Hopelessness. But there's nothing about the way time slips away from you, minutes lost staring at the back of a blond child ahead of you on the sidewalk, seconds ticking past while you stand holding a fresh-from-the-dryer T-shirt that your daughter once wore. Brain blank and empty as a dark room, just her name—*Junie Junie Junie*—running in an endless loop of longing.

I don't know how much time had passed with me staring into the open freezer section at the grocery store. Long enough that my face felt numb from cold, not so long that an employee had asked me if I was all right. I wasn't hungry, my appetite having disappeared along with my daughter. All my clothes hanging loose, jeans held up by the jutting bones of my hips. But eating felt like something Junie would want me to do, so I stood, staring blankly at the colorful boxes of frozen dinners. Chicken, pasta, Salisbury steak. Waiting for something to click in my head, tell me which one to reach for.

And then the thing I'd been anticipating, the hand on my shoulder. The tentative voice in my ear. "Hey, are you okay?" But when I turned my head, it was Zach Logan standing there, his brow creased with concern. I let go of the freezer door and took a stumbling step back from him, his hand sliding down my arm and away.

"I'm fine." I waved my fingers toward the freezer. "Nothing sounds good."

"I know," Zach said. "Everything tastes like cardboard to me. But it's important to eat. You have to keep your strength up."

I wondered if he and Cal had gotten together, formulated a script between them to keep me eating. Wondered if Jenny was getting the same pressure to stick a fork in her mouth.

"I hope you came in the back way," Zach said. "There are reporters out front."

When the reporters had first appeared in town, a few days after Izzy's funeral, I hadn't connected them to the murders. Cal had driven me past a clot of them, cameras and microphones and faces full of fake concern, and I'd turned to him, confused. "What's going on? Why do we have reporters here?" The last time I could remember anything newsworthy happening in Barren Springs was when dead fish filled up the river and half the town thought the end days were coming. And even then it was only the local Springfield news who'd shown up.

Cal had glanced at me. "They're here for Junie," he said. "And Izzy." He spoke slowly, like he wasn't sure if my question had been a joke.

"Oh," I said, feeling like a fool. If it had been someone else's kid laid open like a hunted deer, I would have known in an instant what the media was doing here.

I'd managed not to get cornered by the reporters, for the most part. Using the maze of Barren Springs streets to my advantage. The reporters tended to stay close to the businesses clustered along the highway, their news vans crowding the front lots of the laundromat and the now defunct florist. They didn't seem to realize I parked in the tiny alleys behind the stores, came in through the back doors, and left the same way. Just in case, I'd taken to wearing a baseball hat, hair pulled back in a ponytail, when I ran errands. My half-assed attempt at a disguise.

Everyone in town helped, too. Told the reporters they'd seen me heading toward the Dollar General one town over, or had heard I was grabbing lunch at the sub shop, when really I was right inside my apartment waiting for their news vans to drive away. Nothing brought the people of Barren Springs together like disdain for a nosy outsider. Cal said he'd overhead one of the reporters complaining that they'd never been to a place with people so reluctant to see their own faces on the front of a newspaper. Because no one was talking, the stories, so far, had been a rehash of the same brutal facts everyone already knew, mixed with increasingly disparaging descriptions of Barren Springs.

"Thanks for the heads-up." I let the freezer door close without pulling anything off the shelf. "Have the police talked to you lately?" I asked, fishing to see if he knew about Izzy and the older man. I didn't want to be the one to tell him, not if I could help it.

"They came by yesterday," Zach said. "Asking about her cell phone."

"What about it?"

"They didn't find it. With the girls. I guess they got a list of her cell phone activity and she'd been texting to a burner phone."

"Do they know about what?" I asked.

"Not yet. They're waiting on the phone company." Zach crossed his arms, shook his head. "I can't imagine who she would have been texting. We told her a thousand times she wasn't allowed to text or talk to someone we didn't know."

"Did you ever check her phone?" I asked, only realizing how accusatory I sounded after the words left my mouth.

"At first we did every day, but there was never anything but calls and texts to us and a couple of friends. Most of the kids her age didn't have a phone yet." Zach paused, looked away. "But we'd trailed off the last few months. Neither one of us can remember the last time we read through her texts."

"Maybe it wouldn't have mattered," I told him, because he seemed to be waiting for some kind of reassurance. "Maybe it didn't have anything to do with what happened."

Zach nodded, but it was the kind of perfunctory acknowledgment that meant he didn't believe a word I was saying. That was okay; I didn't believe it, either. "It still doesn't seem real," Zach continued. "That they're both gone." He tried to catch my eye, but I looked away. "I keep waiting for them to walk into the kitchen, demanding snacks. Sometimes I swear I can hear them giggling from Izzy's room late at night." He blinked fast, tightened his jaw. "I check Izzy's bed in the morning to see if she might be there. I know it's stupid, but every day I think maybe she will be."

I wasn't sure what he wanted from me. We shared a loss, but I didn't know Zach Logan, not really. We weren't friends. We were barely acquaintances. And unlike him, I understood, down to the marrow of my bones, that my daughter was gone. Now I had one more thing to envy.

. . .

I'd avoided the park since Junie's death, made sure I went the long way to the grocery store or gas station. But after I left Zach in the frozen food aisle and got back in my car without buying anything, I found myself taking a left on Elm and gliding to a stop at the park. It was empty, yellow crime scene tape tied around a tree at the edge of the playground, the other end loose and flapping in the breeze. I got out of the car, made my way across the scrubby grass to the mouth of the cement tunnel where my daughter had died. There was a dark patch in the dirt, a stain that might have been blood soaked into the earth. I put out a hand, steadied myself on the rough surface of the tunnel.

"I had the same reaction," a voice said, and I whipped my head up, saw Jenny Logan sitting on a picnic table to my right, feet resting on the bench. "But then I told myself it wasn't blood."

"Did that help?" I managed.

She shrugged. "Does anything?" She patted the table next to her hip. "You may want to come sit down. You're looking a little green around the gills."

If I didn't know better, I'd think the Logans were following me around, inserting their lives, their grief, into mine. But I wasn't that convinced of my own importance. This was just a small place, everyone bumping up against each other. I crossed to the picnic table and hoisted myself up, the spring chill of the wood worming its way through my jeans into my skin. "I saw your husband at the Piggly Wiggly a few minutes ago."

Jenny gave a wan half smile. "Always dangerous, sending Zach to the store. Even when I give him a list, he always ends up with a random assortment of crap. I was going to go with him, to get out of the house. But at the last second I couldn't do it."

"Too many people asking how you're doing?"

"Yeah." Jenny nodded. "But some days it's not even that. It's Zach. He keeps reading things online, about how to deal with grief. It's like he thinks if he follows the steps, he can instantly make it better. And when it doesn't work, he freaks out, has no idea what to do when I'm crying and losing my mind. It gets exhausting, you know? Acting like things aren't as bad as they are so he doesn't fall apart. I needed a break."

I didn't know. I guessed that was one benefit of being alone in the aftermath. I didn't have to keep my chin up for someone else, could let myself sink as dark and deep as I pleased.

Jenny leaned back, using her hands behind her for balance, and tipped her face up, eyes closed. She was more disheveled than I was used to seeing her, hair tangled and a little greasy at the roots, dark smudges under her eyes, her shirt wrinkled. Even her speech was looser, words flowing easier off her tongue. Was I seeing her differently since my talk with Cal, aware, suddenly, of the chip on my shoulder? Or maybe Jenny had always been more human than I'd given her credit for and I hadn't had any good reason to notice it before now.

"I wasn't going to come back here, to Barren Springs, after college, did you know that?" she asked without opening her eyes.

Pondering Jenny Logan's life choices wasn't a topic I'd ever spent much time on, but she didn't need me to answer, kept right on talking.

"It wasn't even something I really thought about, never said to myself, 'You're getting out of Barren Springs and never looking back.'" She gave a watery laugh and opened her eyes, leaned forward again. "But it was a given. I thought I'd go to Mizzou, get a degree, then move to Kansas City or St. Louis, someday maybe Chicago."

I didn't really care about this story, about Jenny Logan's life, but I liked focusing on someone else for a change. It felt like a vacation from my own buzzing brain. "What happened?"

"Have you ever left here?" she asked instead of answering my question.

I shook my head. I'd been to Branson once, years ago, for a day. That was the extent of my travels. All I really remembered of it was the bumper-to-bumper traffic, the sea of tourists crowding the sidewalks. How foreign and far away it felt from the quiet green of home. I'd been thinking about moving with Junie, trying to claw our way up in the world. I could have made a little more money there, working at a chain restaurant instead of the diner. But everything else would have cost more, too. At the end of the day, I would've still been poor, still been scraping by. Only I would have been poor in a place without Cal, without Louise and Thomas, without the safety net of Barren Springs—where every square inch was familiar. Branson was a life I couldn't picture for myself, no matter how hard I tried.

"I thought I would love it. All those new people, new experiences." Jenny picked at a thread on her jeans. "But it turns out the world is *big*. Even a place as small as Columbia felt overwhelming. I didn't know who to talk to or how to act. I spent almost every day of those two years desperate to get back here. I remember one night

I got a flat tire and no one on the highway stopped to help me. I was standing out there in the rain, trying to change my tire, sobbing like a baby and thinking that if I were in Barren Springs, if I were *home*, I would've had ten people stopping to help me." She cocked her eyebrows at me. "Can you believe that shit? What a goddamn wimp."

She wasn't wrong, though. That was the thing about Barren Springs; for all its ugliness, there was hidden beauty, too. The way people relied on each other when things got bad, the resourcefulness of a community that most of the world ignored, the sheer stubborn willfulness that kept people breathing when it might have been easier to give up. The rolling hills and the wind in the trees. I had to remind myself of those things on the days I wanted to burn the whole place to the ground.

"When I met Zach and then got pregnant, it seemed like the perfect excuse to drop out of school and come home. Maybe part of me even planned it that way. And God love him, Zach never uttered a word of protest, even though he'd always wanted to move to a big city, get a job at some fancy company. I thought he might resent me for it at some point. But he never has. I'm the one who gets itchy feet sometimes, tries to talk him into moving, and he's the one who wants to stay. God knows why." She glanced at me. "He gave up all his dreams for me and Izzy, and right now I could kill him for it." Her eyes glistened with tears, a few of them spilling over onto her pale cheeks. "I'm furious with him for agreeing to this life because if he hadn't none of this would have happened." She flapped a hand at me. "And I know how unfair and awful that is of me. You don't have to say it."

"I wasn't going to."

That startled a laugh out of her, whisking tears off her cheeks with the backs of her fingers. "You're a breath of fresh air, Eve, honestly. Nothing seems to surprise you."

I shrugged. "It takes more than what you just told me, that's for sure. You're not the only one who looks back after all this and wishes for different choices."

Jenny stared at me like she was trying to unravel my thoughts, crawl inside my brain and fish out the things I wasn't saying. "Like what?" she asked.

"Nothing in particular," I said, eyes drifting away. "Whatever choices led to our daughters dying in this park."

"It wasn't our fault, though," Jenny said, voice small.

"Maybe not," I said, not sounding convincing. "But it definitely wasn't theirs."

Across from the park, a screen door slammed and we both looked up, caught the tail end of Mrs. Stevenson retreating into her house. "God," Jenny said, "you'd think that nosy old bag could have done us a favor and been peering out her front windows when . . ." She gestured toward the tunnel. "She watches this park like a hawk every other day of the year."

"How do we know she wasn't?" I asked.

"Land already talked to her. She said as soon as the snow started, she pulled her drapes and hunkered down. Didn't want to run her furnace in April." Jenny snorted. "Sounds about right. My mom knew her growing up and said she's never met a woman as tight with a dollar. And that's saying something around here."

I squinted into the weak sunlight poking through a tear in the wispy clouds. "You get regular updates from Land?"

"Yeah, pretty regular." Jenny paused. "You don't?" When I shook my head, little plumes of embarrassment flared on her cheeks. "Well, maybe he figured your brother tells you everything anyway."

"Yeah," I said, voice dry. "Either that or he's too busy stuffing his fat ass with doughnuts to bother."

I let my gaze wander the perimeter of the park, but whoever had chosen this spot to go after the girls had chosen well. The Stevenson house was the only one around, and even it was partially obscured by trees. Barren Springs wasn't laid out like the small towns I saw on television, everything extending neatly from a center square. It was almost as if the original settlers hadn't anticipated it ever becoming much of an actual town and so they'd built their houses wherever they pleased, no thought of a master plan. More *every man for himself* rather than a collective endeavor. Streets were added in over time to accommodate the houses, not the other way around, so that some streets had only a single house or ended with no warning. It was a maze of a place, the thick green woods crowding the edges of everything the only constant.

I started to scoot forward, ready to hop down from the table and end this conversation, but Jenny put a hand out, laid it gently on my forearm. "I liked Junie," she said. "I wanted you to know that. Really liked her. Sometimes better than my own daughter, if I'm being honest. Izzy was in that awful preteen phase where you never know if you're going to get a hug or an insult." She sighed. "The last six months felt like an endless eggshell walk around her. Was Junie like that with you?"

I settled back on the table, moved my arm out from under her hand. "No."

Jenny smiled a little. "Yeah, that's what I figured. Junie had a . . . gravity about her, I guess is the best way to describe it. She seemed more settled in herself than Izzy. More settled than I was at that age, that's for sure." Jenny elbowed me gently. "Did she get that from you?"

I was stumped by her question. Not because I didn't have an answer but because I didn't know how to explain it to her. As a child, I'd had Junie's seriousness about life and my place in it because I learned early that to be frivolous, to take things for granted around my mama, was asking for a world of hurt. I hoped that Junie's gravity came from somewhere else entirely, that it was because she was born a little wiser than other babies, a little surer of herself, more secure in the love I always, always gave her. "I don't know," I said finally. "I'd better get going before the reporters figure out where we are."

"This was nice," Jenny said as I made a second attempt to slide off the table. "Spending time with someone who gets it. It's a relief." I understood what she meant. Losing a child the way we had resulted in instant isolation. After the initial flurry of sympathy, people gave you a wide berth in case your bad luck, the dark cloud of murder and violence you lived under, seeped over onto them. She smiled at me as I stood. "Why did we never do this before? Our girls were so close and this is the first time we've ever really had a conversation."

I shrugged, looked away. "Just busy, I guess."

"Well, better late than never. Although I think I did most of the talking. Next time, it's your turn, okay?"

I forced my mouth into a half smile. "Okay," I said, knowing, even if Jenny didn't, that there was never going to be a next time.

TWELVE

When a reporter finally cornered me, I had no one but myself to blame. I'd gone to the laundromat as the sun was rising, hoping to get my laundry done and be back at the apartment before anyone else was stirring. My luck held when I let myself in through the screen door in the back of the laundromat, the smell of perfumed dryer sheets smacking me in the face, and not a single other person in sight. A couple of dryers were full of clothes someone hadn't bothered to pick up from the day before, but all six washing machines were empty. I filled one with whites, the other with everything else, feeding quarters into the slots without really paying attention, my eyes roaming over the bulletin board behind the machines. Notices about yard sales, offers to babysit with phone numbers scrawled on paper tags no one had pulled off, pleas for the return of lost dogs, and there, in the middle, a picture of Junie's face.

It was like taking a punch to the gut, completely unprepared for the sharp stab of pain. I flinched as I stared at her gap-toothed smile, her freckled nose, a number for anyone with tips to call printed below. I fought against the sudden urge to rip down the flyer, to hide her away where other people couldn't gawk at her. I didn't want her to belong to the whole world. I wanted her to still be only mine.

Behind me, the screen door opened on a squeal of hinges and then banged shut again. I stepped away from the washing machines, tugging my baseball cap lower on my forehead. From the corner of my eye, I saw a woman approach, lugging a canvas bag of laundry behind her.

"Morning," she said.

"Hi." I busied myself gathering up my detergent and extra quarters with my back to her, tossing everything into my empty laundry basket for a quick getaway. I knew already that she wasn't from around here. Not enough twang in her vowels, too many expensive highlights in her hair.

"Is there anywhere in town to get coffee this early?" she asked my back. I could hear her opening a washing machine, the clink of quarters.

"The Bait & Tackle, about half a mile down." I gestured west without turning around, waiting for her to start loading in her dirty clothes so I could slip out behind her.

She sighed. "Guess I should have grabbed some at the motel before I left this morning." The nearest motel was five miles east of here, next to a gas station and not much else. Filled now with reporters, which confirmed the sinking feeling in my gut. "I gotta ask, is there anything to do around here, or is this it?"

I pictured Barren Springs the way she was seeing it, a sad collection of buildings nestled right up against the highway. Half of them unoccupied, not even hopeful *For Lease* signs in the windows any-more. The ones that were occupied—this laundromat, the general store with its half-empty shelves, the sub shop, a tiny bar, the bank—not exactly shouting *Come on in* to strangers. The Piggly Wiggly a mile outside of the town proper was the biggest draw we had, bringing residents in need of groceries from all over the county. What she would never see was Jackson Creek, where Cal fished in solitude, or the valley near my mama's trailer, the woods so deep and lush you could get lost ten steps in.

"You lived here long?" she asked, her voice waking up, laundry bag forgotten at her feet as I edged around her toward the door. "Because I'm a reporter. Doing a story on the murdered girls and I'd really love to talk to someone who knows this place. Are you inter-ested?" She moved closer to me, ducking her head a little to get a better view of me.

"No," I said, not looking at her. I reached out to push open the screen door, and the air in the room changed, tightened on her quick inhale.

"You're Eve Taggert, aren't you? Junie's mom?" She laid her hand on my arm.

I did look at her then, watched her brown eyes go wide at what-ever she saw on my face. She took her hand away. I shoved the door open with my shoulder, crossed the parking lot, and tossed my laun-dry basket in the trunk. She was waiting for me by the driver's door of my car, blocking me from opening it with her body. "Listen," she said, voice pitched low and even. "I just want to talk. It doesn't even have to be about Junie. It can be about anything. Whatever you want. Don't you have anything to say?"

"Move," I said, when what I really wanted was to slap my daugh-ter's name out of her mouth.

She took a single step backward, not enough for me to open the car door. I knew what my mama would do if she were here. Swing that door wide and send the bitch flying. But I took a deep breath, held on to my temper through sheer force of will, hand tightening on my door frame until my knuckles screamed. "Move," I repeated, fighting to keep my voice calm.

She moved, although I could see it pained her. Having me so close and all to herself and not able to cash in on it. "I'll be at the press conference tomorrow," she called, jogging alongside my car as I pulled out, tires chirping against the gravel of the parking lot. "Maybe by then you'll have something to say."

"Don't count on it," I muttered under my breath. Talking to reporters was for other people. People who could say the right things and make the right faces. That was never going to be me. Yet another thing I couldn't give my daughter. But maybe, by the time this was over, I'd be able to give her something even better.

.   .   .

It had been with reluctance bordering on refusal that I'd agreed to participate in the press conference with Izzy's parents. Land had called me into the station the day after I'd seen Jenny at the park, said the Logans had already agreed. At first I'd said no flat out, said I didn't see what good it would do to have me there. Couldn't Zach and Jenny handle it? If someone knew something, why would having me standing there make them any more likely to talk? They were either going to spill their secrets or they weren't.

But Cal, as he often did, was the one to convince me, his voice patient long after Land had stormed away in disgust. Cal agreed with me that it might not matter, that it might make not a bit of difference to have my brokenhearted face showing up in living rooms across the entire country. But what if it did? he'd asked. And finally, the kicker: *It's something you can do for Junie.* And I saw suddenly, firsthand, how good of a cop he was, sliding in under people's defenses, talking them into doing things that arguably went against their best interests. So smooth and kind you didn't realize you'd been played until it was too late.

And it was definitely too late now, with bright lights shining into my face and sweat slithering down my back underneath my cheap polyester dress. I wished I'd worn my jeans, but at the last minute I'd swung by the thrift store the next town over and grabbed the first dress I'd seen. Too big and an awful shade of brown. My choice was made all the worse by Jenny Logan, chic and sleek in a black pencil skirt and cream blouse, a single strand of pearls around her neck. The fact that they were probably fake made no difference. She looked the part and I didn't, simple as that. She was someone people could sympathize with. I was the poor, dumb hick who probably deserved what happened to me. I knew people were thinking it because I'd already thought it myself.

Land put the three of us in a row, seated behind a table, Zach in the middle. The table was covered with framed pictures of the girls and I was thankful to be behind them. I knew forming a single word would be impossible with Junie's face staring at me.

Land spoke first, from a podium to my right. I tuned him out, kept my eyes down, the brightness of the lights burning into the top of my head. When Zach spoke, I forced myself to look up, turn my head in his direction. A line of sweat had formed along his hairline, thin enough the cameras probably wouldn't pick it up. "We all, all three of us," he said, glancing first at Jenny and then at me, "are begging anyone with information to come forward. Anything you saw that day, please let law enforcement know."

"Even if you think it's nothing," Jenny interjected. "Even if it seems like nothing. Please, please call it in."

Zach squeezed Jenny's hand on the tabletop. "That's right. You never know what might make a difference. What might help us get justice for our daughters. Whoever did this is still out there. None of us, none of our children, are safe until we catch him."

No one spoke for a moment, the room awash with the sound of clicking camera shutters, the rustling of notebooks. I concentrated on the freckles dotting my arms, remembered Junie tracing them with her fingers. She always said my arms were my very own connect-the-dots. I jerked my eyes upward, trying not to squint as I looked out into the field of reporters. "Ms. Taggert," someone shouted. "Is there anything you'd like to say?"

My eyes were adjusting to the lights, and behind the reporters I could see Cal, face tight with tension. Louise was there to his left, her eyes warm with sympathy. I knew it wasn't possible, but it looked like half the town was crammed into the room, necks craning for a glimpse of the action. And behind everyone else, standing right next to the door, was my mother. Nothing about her was either concerned or sympathetic. Her bony arms were crossed, her face pinched. I could practically hear her voice if a reporter stopped to ask her name. *Mind your own fucking business. How's that for a name?* She looked furious, and her fury fired my own. A match to the anger that now simmered always right below the surface.

I'd taken too long to respond and Land started to jump in, pulling the microphone at the podium toward his face. "This has been difficult for everyone, as you can imagine. Ms. Taggert isn't—"

"I can talk," I said, voice hoarse and too loud. The whole room went silent, the whispery undercurrents cut off cold. Next to me,

Zach stiffened, and I saw his hand flex on the tabletop like he was stopping himself from reaching for me. Whether to silence me or comfort me, I had no idea. Knew only that I was beyond either offering.

"Call in your tips," I said. "Talk to the cops. Do all that. And maybe it will help. But I doubt it." I paused, sucked in a shaky breath. I was smart enough to know the anger zinging through my blood like a fast-acting poison was probably misplaced grief, but I didn't care. It felt good. Felt good to feel something that would potentially hurt someone else instead of harming me. "But that doesn't mean whoever did this should be resting easy, thinking they're going to get away scot-free." I pointed out at the cameras, stabbing my finger into the air. "Because I'm going to find you, you sick fuck. And I'm going to tear you apart."

You could practically taste the shock in the air, a split second when no one moved or spoke, and then it was chaos—cameras clicking, reporters shouting questions, flashes exploding in my face. I caught glimpses between the bursts of light. Jenny staring at me like she'd never seen me before, eyes wide. Louise, still as stone while tears tracked down her cheeks. Cal's hand scrubbing at his tired, defeated face. The reporter from the laundromat, cheeks flushed, probably kicking herself all over again that she hadn't gotten me to talk when she'd had the chance. And Land, his forehead mottled deep red as he gripped my arm, pretending to help me stand but really digging his fingers into my skin, bone biting into tendon.

"What the hell was that?" he said, back turned to the crowd. I stared up at him, and something in his face cracked, softened for a moment. "Jesus, Eve." He sighed. "How was that supposed to help?

We're trying to get people to have sympathy for you, for your situation. Not turn off their televisions because you scare the shit out of them."

I thought about all the press conferences I'd seen over the years, parents trotted out for missing kids, killed kids, abused kids. Everyone feels sorry for those parents, those mothers, until they don't. Until the mothers don't cry enough or cry too much. Until the mothers are too put-together or not put-together enough. Until the mothers are angry. Because that's the one thing women are never, ever allowed to be. We can be sad, distraught, confused, pleading, forgiving. But not furious. Fury is reserved for other people. The worst thing you can be is an angry woman, an angry *mother*.

But I *was* angry and I wasn't going to pretend otherwise. I didn't care what people said about me. And if Land actually thought any of this spectacle would make a difference in finding out the truth about who killed Junie and Izzy, then he was even dumber than I thought.

"Get your fucking hands off me," I said, ripping out of his grasp and lurching backward.

Land's mouth dropped open, but I was already turning away, my gaze skipping to the back of the room. My mama was still leaning against the wall, arms still crossed, eyes still cold. But now, she was smiling.

. . .

I'd reached my car, shaking hand on the door handle, when Cal caught up to me. In the distance, I could hear the sounds of the reporters, but they were blocked from reaching the parking lot by a line of deputies, their cameras kept at bay by a wall of bodies. But still they shouted questions: *Eve, do you have any idea who might have done it? What are you going to do if you catch them, Eve?* I wasn't Ms. Taggert to them anymore, I noticed. My cheap dress, my hard eyes, my outburst had stripped away the formalities. They all thought they knew me now, had me pegged.

Cal let me open the door, slide into the driver's seat, before he leaned inside. Made sure to angle himself where even a long-range lens would get only a shot of his back. "Why, Evie?" he asked, voice quiet. "What in the hell was going through your head?"

"Did you see Mama?" I asked, eyes straight ahead. An early-spring butterfly batted against my windshield, yellow wings flapping.

"What are you talking about?"

"She was there, in the back."

Cal shook his head. "No, I didn't see her." He paused, reached out a careful hand and laid it on my shoulder. "Please don't tell me you're taking cues from Mama now."

"Would it be so bad if I was?"

Cal's hand jerked away. "Hell yes, it would be," he said. When I looked at him, his face was red.

"Why?" I demanded. "She never let anyone get away with anything. She made people pay when they did wrong by us."

A short, harsh laugh gusted out of my brother. "Are you high right now? You been into Mama's stash? Because it sounds like you're forgetting all the times she used us as punching bags. All the times she smacked us around, forgot to feed us, told us we were worthless." He scrubbed at his face with one hand, a sure sign he was exhausted and nearing the end of his rope. "I have no idea where this is coming from. I swear to God, Evie, sometimes lately it's like I don't even know you."

Yeah, I wanted to tell him, *join the club.* "I'm not saying she was a good mother," I said instead. "And you're right, she was never shy about slapping the shit out of us. But no one else touched us. No one dared lift a finger to us. Because they knew what would happen if they did." I jerked my seat belt into position, put my key in the ignition. "I'm just saying, maybe if I'd been more like her, no one would have had the nerve to touch my daughter. Maybe they would have known better."

"Ah, Evie," Cal said, his gentle voice making tears sting the corners of my eyes. "Being more like Mama would have been the worst thing you could have done. For you and for Junie, both."

I thought of my sweet girl, the way she'd snuggle into my side on sleepy Sunday mornings, the way she'd throw her arms around me for hugs, secure in the knowledge I'd always hug her back, press tender kisses to her cheeks. The way she trusted me to never, ever hurt her. Then I thought of her laid out on a metal table, her throat slit open and her life drained away. And I knew that Cal was wrong, because Junie dead, Junie killed, would always be the worst thing of all.

THIRTEEN

After I left Cal in the parking lot, I drove around aimlessly. Snuck out the back exit and watched him fade into a tiny dot in my rearview mirror. I was scared to go straight home, didn't have it in me to be met with a pack of reporters and have to run their gauntlet. Scared of what might come out of my mouth in the seconds between my car and my own front door. I stopped at the Piggly Wiggly and grabbed a handful of Slim Jims and a six-pack of beer, but found my taste for alcohol was still missing, left the first can to warm in my cup holder after a few half-hearted sips. One thing, at least, Cal would be glad to know I wasn't inheriting from our mama.

Finally, because I couldn't think of anywhere else to go, I pulled into the diner's parking lot and backed my car into a spot on the far edge, half hidden in early-evening shadow. Through the plate glass window I caught glimpses of Thomas slinging orders out for pickup, watched Louise and Joan talking to the customers, pouring iced tea and serving pie. I could almost imagine myself in there with them, hollering orders back to Thomas, Junie tucked into the corner booth with her homework spread in front of her, munching on a grilled cheese sandwich while she worked.

I knew Thomas had spotted me, saw his gaze lingering through the window, but when he left for the night, he never once looked my way. Letting me have this time I needed, where I could pretend to be invisible. After he and Joan had gone, I watched Louise wipe down the counters, slide a piece of pie into a Styrofoam container, click off the lights, and lock the door behind her. But instead of walking straight to her car, she crossed the lot to mine. She opened my passenger door and let herself inside, shoved the container at me. "Eat," she said, handing me a fork and shutting the door as she settled into the seat.

"What kind?" I asked.

"Banana cream, all we got left. And don't say you're not hungry."

I knew better than to argue with her, took a dutiful bite. It tasted flat and flavorless on my tongue, and I had to work hard to swallow.

"Thomas told me not to bother you out here, but I couldn't help myself," Louise said. "I've been worried sick about you. And then . . . after today." She paused. "You were the talk of the diner tonight."

"I'm guessing nobody'd seen a press conference like that before."

Louise shifted toward me. "It's not funny, Eve."

"I didn't mean it to be," I said, taking another bite, knowing it was the last one I'd be able to manage.

"It's probably not my place to say this, but someone's got to." Louise twisted her hands together in her lap. "Junie wouldn't have wanted to see you that way. So angry you hardly looked like your-self. It would have broken her heart."

Frankly, I didn't think any of us had any idea what Junie might have wanted. Maybe her fury at being wrenched from the world would have been even greater than mine. Maybe she'd crave blood and revenge. Or maybe she'd want mercy and the mother she remembered. But Junie was gone, and what she would have wanted didn't matter anymore. All that mattered was what I could live with in the aftermath.

I closed the container, the sickly sweet smell of banana threatening to make me gag. "If you're asking me to forgive, I can't do that," I said. "I don't have it in me." Forgiveness was a virtue I'd never been taught and one I didn't have much interest in learning now.

Louise shook her head. "I never said a single word about forgiving. But there's a world of space between forgiveness and vengeance, Eve. A lot of places you can land." She sighed, reached out, and took the container of pie. "I guess two bites is better than nothing."

We sat in silence for a minute, watching the shadows lengthen across the parking lot and listening to the distant sound of a coyote's howl. I leaned my head back and closed my eyes.

"I knew your mama's folks," Louise said into the quiet. "Not well, but your grandma was the same age as my oldest sister. They were friendly, hung around some before your grandma got married."

I opened my eyes and turned my head to look at her. "You've never told me that." My mama never spoke much about her family. All Cal and I really knew was that she'd grown up around here, had a father who'd died when she was young, and had a couple of siblings she hadn't seen or heard from in decades. She didn't like talking about the past, hers or ours. Always said what was done was done, rehashing was a waste of breath.

Louise looked at me with sad eyes. "I was hoping I'd never have to. It's not a happy story, which I guess you could've probably figured out on your own."

"Tell me," I said. I'd learned early not to ask my mama, and eventually I thought I'd stopped caring. But I was suddenly hungry for this history I'd never heard. A background that might help bring my mama's sharp edges into focus.

"Like I said, I didn't know them well. Your grandma was only a teenager when they got married, and after that I didn't have occasion to see her much. Your grandpa had some kind of cabin out in the woods, no running water, outhouse out back. Rough place, even for these parts." Louise shook her head. "He was a mean son of a bitch. Kept to himself, mostly, but he had a reputation. People steered clear."

"Sounds familiar," I said, thinking of how people always gave my mama a wide berth, hoping to be well out of range when she blew.

"But your grandma was a sweet little thing. I think she probably had some romantic idea when she married him. Thought she might civilize him." Louise paused. "But he ground her down into nothing. I'd see her in town from time to time over the years, and she was like a shadow, eyes down, skittish, thin as a rail. Dragging your mama and her other two behind her."

I thought of women I'd seen over the years, bodies constantly hunched for a blow. Thought of myself when Jimmy Ray had been around. "My mama had a brother and a sister, right?"

Louise nodded. "Your mama was the youngest. Her brother ran off when he was about fifteen. Never seen hide nor hair of him again. The sister, Tanya, ended up like your grandma. Married to some man who treated her worse than an old stray dog. They moved away years ago. Don't know what became of them, but I can imagine."

"I know my grandpa died when my mama was young. What happened to my grandma?"

Louise looked away. "No one knows. She just stopped coming into town. Your grandpa claimed she'd run off at some point, but rumor was he'd finally gone too far and beat her to death. Thrown her body in the woods somewhere."

I swear, I sometimes thought there were more bodies tossed in the woods around Barren Springs than had ever been buried in the town cemetery. "And the cops didn't do anything?"

"What was there to do? There wasn't any proof he'd killed her. And it was different back then. People left family matters to families. Your mama'd always been a sharp-eyed little girl. But after your grandma disappeared, she was hard as nails. Looked like she'd rip you to shreds if you so much as touched her. And then, a few years later, your granddad died of that stomach cancer. Your mama was about Junie's age and totally alone in the world. People around town tried to help her, show her some kindness, but she was like a feral animal. All teeth and claws and biting anyone dumb enough to reach out a hand. I know social services got called at some point, but your mama was wily. She knew the holler like the back of her hand, knew people she could hunker down with, places to hide, favors to ask. Somehow, she made her way."

It wasn't hard for me to imagine my mama surviving alone. She'd been doing it since I'd known her. One of those rare creatures who didn't seem to need much of anything, not love or money or a purpose, to keep on breathing.

Louise shifted in her seat so she could look straight at me. "When something like that happens to a person, it either shapes them or it breaks them. And God love her, your mama didn't break, I can say that much for her. Most people would have. But your mama saw the way her world worked and she adapted. But she let it shape her into something ugly, let it turn something inside her. Or maybe she was born like her daddy and was always gonna end up this way, I don't know. I still remember the day I saw her in town, her belly all swollen with Cal, and my heart dropped, worrying about what kind of mama she'd turn out to be. And then, years later, you walked into the diner looking for a job, so much like her but not completely gone over yet. Because you had Cal, had someone to keep you afloat. But it wasn't until Junie was born that a light went on in you. Bright as anything." Louise reached over and took my hand, smoothed it between her own. "I didn't tell you this story to make you feel sorry for your mama or to make excuses for her. I told you because I can see how she's pulling at you, making you think her way might be the right way. But it isn't true. Junie may be gone, but you don't have to slide backward, Eve. There's other, better choices."

I let her hold my hand for another minute, kiss me on the cheek as she got out of the car. I promised her I'd think about what she said and that I'd do a better job eating. I said what she needed to hear because I didn't have the heart to tell her that she was too late; I was already at home in the dark.

.   .   .

When I got back to my apartment building, I turned off my engine and waited, listened to the sound of the night: trees rustling in the wind, a man's far-off hollering for a dog or a child, the tinny sound of someone's radio drifting out through their open apartment window. But I didn't hear any reporters, saw no news vans or clicking heels racing over to check who was inside my car. They must have given up and gone to look somewhere else. Maybe they were camped outside the Logans' house, a more picturesque scene, to be sure.

I wasn't sure I had the energy to get out of my car, walk across the parking lot, and climb the flight of stairs to my apartment. Open the door and face the empty rooms that still smelled like my daughter. But falling asleep in my car and being awoken by cameras in my face would have been even worse. Not because I really cared about being captured with drool on my cheek and sleep in my eyes, but because I'd never hear the end of it from Cal. Land, either. There was a protocol to grieving on a national stage and I'd already fucked it up once. I wouldn't be allowed to do it again.

My footsteps made hollow slapping sounds on the concrete steps as I climbed, my steady progress screeching to a halt when I stepped out onto the landing and saw a man sitting in front of my apartment door, knees drawn up and forehead resting on his folded arms. He raised his head when he heard me, stared at me through bleary, beer-heavy eyes.

I crossed my arms across my chest. "What are you doing here?" I'd always taken Junie to Izzy's house, or picked Izzy up at her own. Izzy's parents had never been here. I wasn't aware Zach Logan even knew where I lived.

He'd been crying, the dim light catching silvery trails on his cheeks. "That thing you said today . . ."

I sighed. Louise had been right. Apparently my scene at the press conference was all anyone could talk about. "I shouldn't have said it. Not out loud. I'm sorry I ruined the press conference." I knew how to apologize even when I didn't mean it, knew how to make the right words come out of my mouth in hopes they might diffuse whatever punishment was coming my way. With my mother, sometimes it worked, sometimes it didn't. But other people didn't have her gift for sniffing out insincerity. It was like serving cake without the frosting. I'd left out the most important part, but people ate it anyway.

Zach pushed himself upright, less drunk than I'd originally thought, his movements still fluid and precise. "No," he said. "I'm glad you said it. I'm glad you *feel* it. I'm sick of being sad all the time. Sick of pretending to be strong. I think anger might be a relief."

I shoved past him, slammed my key into the lock on my apartment door. "It's not a relief. None of this is a relief."

When his hand fell on my shoulder, I froze, didn't turn around. "What are you doing?" I whispered. "Go home."

"I don't want to go home," Zach said, voice quiet. "My house doesn't feel the same anymore."

I pushed my door open, shrugged out from underneath his warm hand. I took a deep breath, made my face a blank before I turned to look at him. Close enough that I could smell the beer on his breath and the mint he'd chewed to cover it up, could see the golden starbursts in his brown eyes and the dark stubble forming along his jawline. "Stop it," I said, voice stern, while inside my gut twisted and my heart jumped. "You're acting crazy."

Zach laughed, a hollow bark. "I *feel* crazy." He took a step forward, into my open doorway so I couldn't close him out. "I keep thinking about them. What they went through. How scared they must have been." His voice broke and he swallowed hard. "How I should have been able to save them." He held both hands out, toward me or God or the girls, I had no idea. "What kind of father can't protect his own daughters?"

Something close to terror exploded inside of me, a clawing panic that left my voice weak and reedy when I spoke. "Junie wasn't your daughter."

Zach looked at me, eyes steady, not even a little bit drunk now. "We both know she was."

I stumbled backward, body still upright but the rest of me spinning, sliding into the past even as my brain frantically tried to stay moored in the present. "She was mine," I rasped. "Only *mine*." I realized too late that by stepping back, I'd left Zach room to move inside the apartment, shutting the door behind him. Trapping me. I wasn't scared of Zach himself, but whatever words he said next were going to rip into me like bullets, leave jagged, bloody wounds. And I was already weak, had barely anything left to offer up as a shield.

"It wasn't immaculate conception, Eve," he said. "I was there. She was mine, too." He walked toward me but stopped when I backed away. "You don't know how many times I picked up the phone those first few years, wanting to call. I used to sit right out there in your parking lot at night and debate whether I should knock on your door. But I never did, because you'd asked me not to." He shook his head slightly. "You have no idea how fucking happy I was when Izzy came home from school all those years ago talking about her friend Junie. Asking if she could have her over to play. I couldn't say yes fast enough. The first time Junie came around, I spent the whole day staring at her. I'd seen the two of you from a distance, but I never knew she had freckles or what her laugh sounded like. I was worried Jenny would figure it out from the way I watched her."

"Does she know?" I managed. "Jenny?"

"No." Zach shook his head. "Not a clue." He looked toward Junie's alcove, gestured with his hand. "Can I?"

I didn't respond. Couldn't. I wanted this to all be a bad dream, something I could shake away in the morning light. In my mind, Junie didn't have a father, had simply emerged from me, part of my body and no one else's. I watched, silent, as Zach stepped into Junie's room. He sucked in a quick breath, threw me a pained smile over his shoulder. "Smells like her," he said. A scream built in my head, pounding against my skull as he touched her quilt, ran his hand over her bedside table, picked up one of her textbooks and balanced it in his hand. "I was always good at science. And she was, too. We talked about it sometimes when she was at our house. Izzy never quite grasped it, but Junie did." He set down the book. "Maybe she got that from me."

I turned and walked into the kitchen, my breathing shallow and too fast, vision spinning. Banana cream pie climbing back into my throat. I didn't turn around, even when Zach's footsteps stopped behind me, his body close enough that I could feel his exhales stir the tiny hairs at the nape of my neck.

"You told them you hadn't seen me since that night," he said quietly.

"What?" I sounded like I was sprinting, lungs tight as I tried to outpace something determined to sink its claws into me.

"At the funeral home that first night. With Land. You said you hadn't seen Junie's father since the night she was conceived." He ran one finger down the back of my neck, and my entire body pulsed. "You lied."

I spun around, startling him enough that this time he was the one to take a step backward. But still too close to me. "I didn't lie."

"Yes, you did. Because I've been right here, Eve, all this time. All these years."

"No. Zachary Logan has been here all this time. With his button-down shirts and his boat dealership and his pretty wife and daughter." I stabbed into his chest with my finger, snatched my hand away the second I made contact. "I don't know that guy. I don't recognize him. He's nothing to me." I reached behind me and grabbed the counter with both hands, steadying myself. "I didn't lie," I repeated.

"Okay," Zach said, with a little smile. "Omitted, then." He closed the distance between us, his body almost pressed up against mine. "You recognize me now?" he asked, voice soft.

I looked at him, really looked at him, in a way I hadn't in years. Letting my eyes linger instead of skipping over him like a busted needle on a record player, getting only the vaguest impression before moving on. And tonight he was as close to my memory as he'd ever been, with his dark hair tousled and messy, his faded blue T-shirt, his smell of sweat and aftershave. He looked real to me for the first time in years.

"Do you?" he asked again.

"Yes," I whispered.

When he kissed me, it was like tumbling off a cliff. Falling head-first into the past. Time unspooling in reverse so that we both were impossibly young again, Junie a speck on some future horizon we hadn't even imagined yet. And we tore at each other as if we could somehow start over, re-create what had already happened and make it turn out differently this time around, undo what had already been done.

But in the end, with my lips swollen from his mouth, his back marked by my nails, nothing had changed. It was too late. We were still strangers. And our daughter was still dead.

FOURTEEN

I might have lied to Land about never having seen Junie's father again, but the rest of the story was true. It *was* a fuck-and-run. A one-night stand. No-strings-attached sex. It was all those things, but more than that, too. Even before the reality of Junie was born, that night was always more than its on-paper definition.

Sunday nights at the diner were slow. Dinner service stopped at five, and only drinks and desserts were available until the doors closed at eight. It was the only night Thomas ever got a break, and he always drove away at five o'clock on the dot, leaving a single waitress to man the diner. It was a shit shift, no tips because there were never more than a couple of customers, at most. Because I was the newest waitress, hired at the start of summer, I was the one working that sticky mid-July night when Zach Logan walked through the door.

I'd never seen him before, glanced through the plate glass window and realized I'd never seen his dark blue SUV, either. He wasn't from around here, which made him instantly interesting. And his looks didn't hurt, either. Slow half smile when he saw me, hair ruffled from the wind, slight farmer's tan on his neck where his T-shirt pulled away from his skin. "You open?" he asked, swinging onto a counter stool before I answered.

"We close in five minutes," I told him. I'd never been shy, but I moved through life with a certain watchfulness, wary of unexpected movements, faces. But something about him drew me closer. I was almost amused, observing myself from a distance. So *this* was attraction. I'd slept with a half dozen guys already, had endured untold numbers of sloppy make-out sessions behind the school or in the woods near my mama's trailer. Always waiting for that buzzing in my belly, that heat in my cheeks that happened to other people. And here it was. Came sauntering right through the diner door when I'd least expected it.

I served him a piece of key lime pie and a cup of lukewarm coffee, locked the front doors and put out the *Closed* sign while he ate. Accepted his invitation to sit next to him, tried not to notice the way the tiny hairs on my arm stood up every time his hand brushed against my skin while we talked.

He told me he was about to start his senior year in college, that he was from Illinois, passing through Barren Springs. On his way to somewhere better, I'd assumed. Chicago, he confirmed, where he had a summer internship. I don't remember what I said in return. Some sterilized version of my own truth. I know I lied about my age, thinking that seventeen seemed too young to his twenty-one, might make him skittish and not likely to act on the spark I saw in his eyes. Not dumb enough to believe I'd ever see him again, but still wanting this moment, this night. This boy who didn't belong here, a piece of something that was foreign and different and just for me. A boy who didn't know my mama or my history. A boy who hadn't already written my entire story the second he laid eyes on me.

When I got up to turn off the lights, I let him follow me. Welcomed his hand sneaking under my skirt as the diner plunged into semidarkness. Closed my eyes and pretended I had a different life when he kissed me, the taste of whipped cream on his tongue. With him I was simply a girl who liked a boy. I wasn't Cal Taggert's less-attractive sister. I didn't have a fading bruise on my cheek from my mama's backhand. I wasn't destined to spend the rest of my life working in this diner, always poor and always hungry for something more, even if I lacked the drive to reach for it. For those few hours, I let go of myself, and I was someone new.

When he drove away, sometime after midnight, I had no expectation of ever seeing him again. I didn't pine for him, or daydream about what might have been. I'd never been that girl, and one night with Zach hadn't changed that. The real world beyond Barren Springs had swallowed him up, taillights fading into the dark, and I'd stayed behind. And that's the way it was always going to be. I didn't waste time wishing for a different ending, even after I held the positive pregnancy test in my hand.

But, of course, I did see him again. Six months later. I'd gotten a weekend job helping serve food at Jenny Sable's wedding. Marrying some guy she met at college, apparently. Dropped out and decided to become a Mrs. instead of finishing her degree. Rumor was she had a bun in the oven already, but I didn't pay much attention to the details. Just knew the reception was quite an event for Barren Springs. A buffet *and* passed hors d'oeuvres. Catered from the Blue Lantern, the only halfway-decent restaurant in a fifty-mile radius, and even then most everything came frozen and reheated in a microwave. A blustery, late-January day and 125 guests crammed into the old Elks Lodge on the edge of town. They'd tried to make it nice, hanging fairy lights and stuffing fake flowers into every dark corner, but the whole place still smelled like wet carpet and old cigarette smoke, the fake wood paneling slightly tacky to the touch. "Putting lipstick on a pig," Louise said with a shake of her head when we arrived, both decked out in the matching cheap black dresses Jenny's mom insisted we wear. Mine barely fit over my basketball stomach, and Jenny's mom's mouth pinched in disapproval when she saw me.

I was out in the kitchen, loading lukewarm potato skins onto a platter, when the bride and groom arrived, caught only the tail end of the cheering as I made my way out into the reception hall. The first glimpse I got of Zach was when I offered my tray to a group of men, and he turned to face me, pale pink rose in his tuxedo lapel, shiny gold ring on his finger. I expected him to play dumb, pretend he'd never seen me before. When his face went slack at the sight of me, I wasn't surprised. But I stumbled backward when he reached a hand out toward me, red patches blooming high on his cheekbones when his gaze fell to my stomach. Potato skins slid off my tray, smearing under my heels as I backed away.

I tried to avoid him after that. Kept to the edge of the room, lurking in the shadowiest corners like a ghost. I watched his head swivel, searching, even as he listened to toasts in his honor, took his first spin on the dance floor with his new wife. He wasn't pretending he hadn't seen me, wasn't trying to avoid me. Even as I wished desperately that he would.

Eventually, he caught up with me. It was after the cake cutting, the party in full drunken swing, and I had taken a breather outside.

I leaned back against the ragged brick wall and crossed my arms for warmth. It was cold, my breath steaming in the dark air, but the back of my neck and under my arms were dank with sweat. The baby kicked hard against my ribs, and I rubbed against her foot, willing her to settle down.

I knew it was him the second the door swung open, the sound of laughter and '90s pop music drifting out behind him. "Hey," he said. "I've been looking for you."

I closed my eyes, told myself to get this moment over with. "You didn't need to," I said, without turning my head or opening my eyes. "I'm fine."

I felt him settle in beside me, his shoulder brushing mine as he leaned against the wall. He smelled like flowers from his new wife's bouquet. "How far along are you?" he asked quietly.

I did look at him then. "Are you asking if it's yours?"

He shook his head. "I know it is, from the expression on your face. So six months, right? Give or take a few weeks."

I nodded, brought my hands up to my mouth, and blew on my half-numb fingers. Zach started to shrug out of his tuxedo jacket, but I stopped him, put a hand on his arm. "No, don't. If someone comes out, it won't look right."

Zach laughed at that, but it was a sharp, hard sound. "That's the least of my worries right now."

"I'm not asking you for anything," I told him. "I don't expect anything. You should go back in."

Zach turned sideways, braced his shoulder against the wall. I didn't like him staring right at me, his body close to mine. "What are you going to do?" He reached out, his splayed fingers hovering above the curve of my belly. I shifted away and he dropped his arm.

"I'm going to finish my senior year." I shrugged. "And then I'll work full-time at the diner. I'll figure it out." It had never occurred to me to do anything other than have the baby. It was what the women I knew did. No matter how many came along or how little time or money there was to care for them, babies were born around here. It had nothing to do with the faded billboards that lined the highway warning that abortion stops a beating heart, photo of a tiny fetus curled up like a tadpole. Hell, my mama would have spit in the face of anyone who told her she had to give birth, anyone who thought they had any right to tell her what to do, or not to do. But it was also a fact that getting rid of either Cal or me had never crossed her mind.

"You're in high school," Zach said, not a question, more of a hor- rified realization, his eyebrows crawling up toward his hairline. "Je- sus Christ. You didn't tell me that." He ran a hand through his hair, mussing up the strands.

"Yeah, well, you told me you were passing through. Never heard you mention the girlfriend you had stashed down the road."

He gave me a weak half smile. "We're both liars, I guess."

"I prefer *omitters*," I said, and his half smile turned into a real one, warm and bright. My heart squeezed in my chest.

Zach's smile faded. "For the record, Jenny broke up with me that weekend I met you. We got back together soon after, but I wasn't cheating, for what it's worth."

I nodded, and a loud cheer went up on the other side of the wall, the music swelling against our backs. "It's getting crazy in there," I said. "You're missing your own party."

"I'm not going to disappear," Zach said. "You're not in this alone."

"Yes, I am." I held up a hand when he started to speak. "And that's okay. You have a life and there's no point in screwing it up. It's not like you and I were ever going to be a long-term thing."

"If I'd known . . ."

Now it was my turn to smile. "What? You wouldn't have married Jenny? You'd have married me instead? Come on. We don't even know each other."

He didn't argue with me, but he didn't go back inside, either. "You want me to walk away?" He reached out again and this time put his hand on my belly before I could deflect him. The baby kicked out hard, probably because my whole body tightened up at the contact. Wonder exploded on Zach's face, and when he looked at me, I could see the sadness in his eyes. "Do you know what it is?"

I shook my head. "No. But I think it's a girl."

"I want to know this baby," he said as he pulled his hand away.

I pictured it for a split second. Having someone to help with the bills, someone to hold the baby when I was tired, someone to share the burden. But just as quickly I pictured the look on Jenny's face when she found out. The look on her mother's. The talk that would follow my child, the anger, the shame. Being a single, out-of-wedlock mother was nothing new around here. But fucking Jenny Sable's new husband, forcing him to become a father before Jenny managed to squeeze out a baby herself? That would haunt us forever.

I pushed away from the wall. "You'll have your own babies soon enough. And then you'll be glad not to have to deal with this one. Like I said, we'll be fine."

"Hey, wait," Zach said, snagged my hand as I moved past him. "If you ever change your mind, and I mean *ever*, I'm right here. An hour from now, next week, next month, next year. Anytime." He squeezed my fingers. "You know where to find me."

I didn't believe him, not really. No one would willingly let some-one implode their life. I had a pretty strong inkling that if I showed up on Zach Logan's doorstep a year from now, our baby clutched in my arms, he'd march my ass right back down his front walk and deny ever having met me. But the fact that he'd made the offer warmed me. He was a good man, or at least was trying to be one. If I was going to get knocked up by a stranger, I could have done a lot worse.

I had thought that was the end of it. And for a long time, it was. Until first grade when Junie came home talking about her new friend Izzy, how they both had double-jointed fingers and a birth-mark on their elbows. Asking with pleading eyes if she could spend the night at Izzy's house. *Please, Mama, please, please, please.* And I realized some things will always find their way back to you, no mat-ter how much you wish they'd stay lost.

FIFTEEN

My mama was the last person I expected at my front door the next morning. When the pounding first started, I thought, *Reporters*. And then, right on the heels of that thought, *Jenny*. She'd spied those scratches on Zach's back and was coming over to remark her territory. I was braced for a fight I had no interest in winning when I swung open the door, then stood shocked into momentary stillness when my mama marched into my apartment and kicked the door shut behind her. She looked me up and down, shook her head. "At least you aren't still wearing that potato sack from yesterday. Good God, girl, did you *try* and find the ugliest dress in the store?"

Given her torn jean shorts and too-small T-shirt emblazoned with a faded skull and crossbones, I didn't think she had much room to give fashion advice. But I kept my mouth shut, made my weary way toward the kitchen to start the coffee maker.

"What are you doing here?" I asked. She hadn't been inside my apartment since before Junie's birth. Had come sniffing around when I was eight months pregnant and barely moved in; Cal paying the first month's rent for me so I could escape the trailer before the baby was born. I'd told her then she wasn't welcome in my life anymore, but she'd still shown up at the hospital, drunk and smelling like sex, when Junie was only a day old. Raking me over the coals for not giving birth in the trailer, called me a stuck-up bitch, a weak, spoiled brat thinking I was too good for the midwife who had brought both me and Cal into the world. Ranting loud enough that security had come to escort her away. That had been the first and last time she'd been in the same room with my daughter.

She slid into one of my kitchen chairs, pulled out a cigarette, and lit up without asking permission. "Is that any way to talk to me?" she said.

I sighed, pulled two mugs down from the cabinet above the sink. I wasn't in the mood for her games, her back-and-forth. I'd had to endure it as a child, but I was a grown-up now. "What do you want, Mama?"

"Surprised you're up this early." She took a long drag on her cigarette, and smoke billowed from her nostrils. "Seeing as how you had a late-night visitor."

I froze in the act of pulling milk out of the fridge, kept my head turned away where she couldn't see my face. "What are you talking about?"

I didn't have to see her to hear the smirk in her voice. "That Izzy Logan's daddy. Walked out of here like he was half drunk. And not on alcohol." She gave a guttural laugh. "Let me guess, he was looking for a certain kind of *comfort*." She let her voice linger on the word, making it sound dirty and disgusting. And to most of the world that's what it would be. A married man and his baby mama, hooking up in her crappy apartment while his grieving wife sat at home alone. But there was so much more to the story. It had never been about the sex. It had been about Junie. And this morning Zach was back where he belonged.

"You don't know what you're talking about," I muttered. When I poured coffee into my mug, it slopped over, scalding my fingers. "Ow, shit." I flapped my hand. "What were you doing here last night anyway?" Hoping to deflect her attention, already knowing it was a losing battle. When she latched on to something, sensed a weakness, she was worse than a dog with a bone.

"Came to see you. But changed my mind when I saw Logan do-ing the walk of shame." She got up and wet a paper towel in the sink, held out her hand for mine and wrapped my fingers in the cool cloth. I used my free hand to point at the oval scar on the back of my hand, below the edge of the paper towel. "Remember that?" I asked her.

She nodded. "Yep. You had it coming." No remorse, no give. I'd been seven and whining for dinner, not shutting up even when she'd warned me. Cal must not have been home; otherwise he would have stopped me, pulled me away before things went bad. But he hadn't been there, and Mama'd grabbed the white-hot spoon she'd been using to melt meth and held it to the back of my hand. It was the one constant of my childhood. A refrain as familiar as my own name. *You had it coming.* Four easy words that excused every variation of sin. Thanks to Louise, I knew more about my mama's past now, but it didn't do a single thing to change our present. Even if I wanted a different relationship between us, even if I tried, she never would, because she saw absolutely nothing wrong with everything that had come before.

I started to pull my hand away, and she tightened her grip. "Logan is Junie's daddy, isn't he?" she asked.

"No," I said.

She tsked at me under her breath. "I'm not gonna tell no one, if that's what you're worried about. I can keep my mouth shut with the best of 'em."

My shoulders slumped, and I leaned back against the counter, all the fight, all the denial, gone out of me. "How'd you know?" Someone finally figuring it out, after all this time, didn't feel like the relief I'd thought it might.

My mama shrugged, let go of my hand. "A feeling I got when I saw the two of you at the press conference. The way he looked at you."

I shook my head. "He doesn't look at me any sort of way."

"Yeah, he does. Man's got a soft spot for you. I could see it clear as day. Then something about the way he swung his arms when he walked. Reminded me of Junie." She shrugged again. "Put two and two together, that's all."

See? That's what I mean about never underestimating my mama. Doesn't matter how many drugs she does or how worthless she appears to be. She's always watching. Calculating. Filing things away. She always has exactly the right ammunition at exactly the right moment. And before you know what's happening, you wind up ambushed and gut-shot, my mama standing over you, triumphant.

"Well, at least I know who Junie's father actually is," I told her. "Gives me a leg up on you."

My mama blew air out from between pursed lips. "Doesn't mat-

ter who he was. I don't care. He was only a sperm donor anyway."
Typical Mama. Trying to shame her always backfired because it was
an emotion she couldn't feel. As a kid, I'd tried every which way to
get her to tell me about my father. I even tried crying once, always
a dangerous tactic with Mama, more likely to get you smacked than
comforted. I told her kids at school were making fun of me. She'd
pinched me hard enough to break skin, told me to shut my lying
mouth before she shut it for me. Said she knew none of those kids
gave two shits about who my daddy was because most of them
didn't have a daddy, either. For a long time, I'd nurtured the thought
she was hiding some big, dark secret. Like maybe my daddy was
famous and she'd been sworn to secrecy. But eventually I'd wised
up and realized Mama was telling the truth. She had no idea who
he was, probably couldn't even pick him out of a lineup.

"You still haven't said why you were here last night," I reminded
her. "What you needed to talk to me about."

She flapped her hand like whatever it was barely mattered. "Was
gonna tell you to go talk to Marion." She poured the remains of her
coffee into the sink. "But make sure you've got some time to kill.
That woman ain't never told a story she can't manage to drag out
half the day."

I cocked my head. I saw Marion whenever I went into the Bait &
Tackle, but I couldn't imagine what in particular she'd want to dis-
cuss with me. "Talk to Marion about what?"

"That guy Izzy'd been fooling around with."

"Wait, what . . ." I felt about ten steps behind. "How'd you know
about that?"

My mama smiled, showed off her yellow teeth. "Same way I know
about everything, Eve. I pay attention."

. . .

My mama doesn't really have friends. Not the kind you're thinking of, anyway. No one she goes to lunch with or tells her secrets
to. No one she can count on when the chips are down. But if she
was pressed to name a friend, Marion is probably who she'd pick.
They've known each other their whole lives, from what I can gather.
To say they like each other might be stretching the truth. I've heard
my mama bitch about Marion more often than she's praised her. But
they're cut from the same cloth, honor the same code. Stick together, don't snitch, hit first, and hit hard. They understand each
other, my mama and Marion.

I didn't see Marion as often as I used to, when she was a frequent
visitor to my mama's trailer. Her family had owned the falling-
down Bait & Tackle for generations, but it was a place I generally
tried to avoid—dark, cramped, and smelly. I only set foot inside
when I was desperate for some essentials and both the Piggly Wiggly and the general store were closed. I always swore a half gallon
of milk from the Bait & Tackle left an aftertaste of rotten fish in
your mouth. Buying anything there made you feel poor and dirty.
The Bait & Tackle might have been an institution around here, but
anybody who could afford it drove ten miles down the road to buy
their hooks and worms somewhere else.

The one constant inside the store, besides the smell, was Marion
herself. She held court from behind the cracked counter, an ancient
cash register on one side of her and an overflowing, ceramic ashtray
on the other. My mama smokes, but Marion *smokes*. Takes after a
carton of cigarettes like it's her job. So it wasn't exactly a shock to
find her puffing away on an unfiltered Marlboro when I stepped
through the door.

"Well, good goddamn," Marion said, loud. "Is that little Evie Taggert I spy?"

"Hi, Marion," I called, picking my way past buckets writhing with worms.

"Don't mind those," Marion said. "Fucking Earl Willows thinks he's gonna get rich digging up half his backyard and bringing it in here. Man's a moron." She shook her head, tapped a long cylinder of ash off her cigarette. "How you been, girl?"

"Oh, you know," I said, looking away.

"Not good, is what I'm guessing. Some kind of bullshit, what happened to your Junie."

In other places, the murder of two little girls would have blanketed the entire town in horror. Here, it was just another bad day. I hesitated, not sure of the appropriate response, before finally settling on a half-hearted "Yeah, it was."

"You hungry?" Marion asked. "'Cause I got a vat of that roadkill chili in back. Little spicy this time, but you're welcome to a bowl."

Marion's chili was the stuff of legend, and I'd eaten a hundred bowls of it in my lifetime. When I used to come in here with Junie, she'd try hard not to wrinkle up her nose at the sight of it. Said she couldn't imagine slurping down a spoonful of tire-flattened raccoon or squashed opossum. She was worried she'd barf before she got it swallowed and then Marion would smack her on the back of the head the way she did the boys who tried to steal Slim Jims off the counter. It had always made me a little proud that Junie refused the chili. Proof she wasn't so hungry she'd eat anything to fill her belly. Tangible evidence that I was a better mama than my own.

"No thanks. No chili for me today."

Marion eyed me over the new cigarette she was lighting. "What's brung you my way? I'm not exactly a regular stop." Her voice was friendly enough, but her eyes were hard. She knew I wanted something from her, wasn't there to shoot the shit or buy a loaf of bread. And familiarity didn't buy me any special favors. Another way Marion was like my mama. You had to earn every scrap.

I sidled closer to the counter. The shop looked empty, but someone could be lurking in one of the shadowy corners, listening. I leaned on the ancient floor freezer, the glass coated with a sheen of dirty frost and inside gutted fish stacked right next to freezer-burned popsicles and stale ice cream sandwiches. "My mama told me you might know something about Izzy Logan." I paused. "And the man she was seeing."

"Did she now?" Marion shook her head. "Not like your mama to be running her mouth."

Frustration rose up in me, a black, swamping wave. I didn't have time for this bullshit. To jump through Marion's hoops. My daughter was dead, and people could either get on board and help me or get the hell out of my way. "Are you going to tell me or not?"

Marion blew a plume of smoke in my direction. "Yeah, I'll tell you." She reached out and snagged my wrist in her hand, tightened her fingers until I winced. "But don't go getting too big for your britches, you hear? I tell your mama how you talked to me, and she's liable to teach you a lesson on respecting your elders."

I stared back at her until she dropped my wrist. "I'll take my chances."

I don't know what I expected, but Marion's big booming laugh definitely wasn't it. "Well, look at you," she hooted. "I thought maybe that mouth of yours was gone for good."

"Nope," I told her. "Just been in hiding." That mouth one more thing I buried when Junie was born. Wanting to teach her a better way to approach the world. One that wouldn't leave her judged as poor white trash and not much else. But now I wondered if maybe a mouth like I used to have might have helped save her. Maybe she'd have been more likely to scream. To tell someone to go fuck themselves. To fight back. Or maybe it would have only made the knife move faster. Truth is, there's no good way to navigate being female in this world. If you speak out, say no, stand your ground, you're a bitch and a harpy, and whatever happens to you is your own fault. *You had it coming.* But if you smile, say yes, survive on politeness, you're weak and desperate. An easy mark. Prey in a world full of predators. There are no risk-free options for women, no choices that don't come back to smack us in the face. Junie hadn't learned that yet. But she would have, eventually. We all do, one way or the other.

Another snort from Marion. "In hiding. You always did have a way with the words, even when you was little."

I drummed my knuckles on the countertop, something gritty sticking to my skin. "Izzy?" I prompted.

Marion took another drag from her cigarette. "Getting right down to business. I can respect that." She paused, pointed at me with one nicotine-stained finger. "Don't ask me how I know because I ain't gonna tell you." She swirled her cigarette through the air. "A magician never reveals her secrets."

"I won't ask," I said, trying to hurry her along. My God, she loved an audience. My mama was right about that.

Marion leaned forward. "She was seeing that Matthew fellow. The one works for Jimmy Ray. Has that stupid-looking ponytail. Heard she was like a cat in heat around him."

"Matt?" I said, momentarily struck dumb. The bartender from the strip club. The absolute asshole. The worst of all possible bad choices. *Oh, Izzy, what were you thinking?* "How did they even meet?"

"Got no idea," Marion said. "Figured they crossed paths at some point, liked what they saw. Don't know how far it had gone or nothing like that. But I have it on good authority that he wasn't exactly telling her no."

"She was twelve."

Marion shrugged. "And he's an asshole with a pecker. This shouldn't be news to you. It's the oldest story in the world."

I wanted her to be wrong. I wanted to live in a world where grown men didn't prey on twelve-year-old girls. But she was right, of course. It was nothing new. Nothing that wasn't done every second of every day in every corner of the world. Little girls were never safe. I should know; I used to be one of them.

SIXTEEN

Originally Barren Springs had been a dry town in a dry county, the band of ragtag settlers still determined to put God first in thanks for his having saved them from starvation and ruin. Their resolve hadn't lasted long; soon as folks figured out how rough life was around here—discovered that just because land is pretty doesn't make it farmable—they realized liquor was vital to take the edge off, make the days bearable. But most of the drinking in Barren Springs was still done in private, as if God wouldn't count it against you so long as you didn't throw it in his face. Beer bought at the Piggly Wiggly and consumed by the case down by the creek or flasks of whiskey tucked under car seats for swigs on the way home from work. Other than Jimmy Ray's strip joint, the only watering hole in Barren Springs was Cassidy's, a tiny bar wedged between the laundromat and the questionable sub shop. It had a leg up on Jimmy

Ray's place because it served a couple of actual cocktails and smelled like dryer sheets instead of strippers. Of course, at least half the town would say those were knocks against it. I'd only been inside a handful of times, mainly with Louise, whose husband, Keith, worked the bar most nights. Cassidy's only held about thirty people at capacity, the space long and narrow. Bar running the length of the right side, liquor bottles always shaking slightly when the dryers on the other side of the shared wall were in full spin, and a few two-top tables lining the left. Tonight, at half an hour before closing on a Tuesday, there was only one man bellied up to the bar and Keith cleaning up behind it.

"Hey, sweetheart," Keith said when I came through the door, sweatshirt thrown over my pajamas and flip-flops on my feet. "Hated to bother you, but I didn't want him driving. I tried to get his keys, but he wouldn't hand them over."

Keith's call had woken me from the first deep sleep I'd had in what felt like years. Actual slumber, not simply skimming the surface of rest with thoughts of Junie floating against my closed eyelids. "It's okay," I said. "How long's he been here?"

"Most of the night," Keith said. He was wiping down the bar and paused where Cal's head rested on the wood. "Poor fucker. I think it all caught up with him. I wasn't gonna bother you, but the usual suspects were sniffing around. Brenda Longmont, that Candy girl you went to school with. I figured he was gonna have enough regrets in the morning, didn't need to add waking up next to one of them to the list."

"Yeah," I said. "Good call." I slid onto the stool next to Cal's, ran my hand over his hair. "Hey, Cal. Come on, wake up."

Cal had never been a drinker, not even when we were younger and I was a little too friendly with the bottle. He'd watched our mama and went the other way, a decision I mimicked as soon as I got pregnant. But while I'd given up drinking for good, Cal still had the occasional beer after work or while watching the game. But I'd only seen him really drunk once before, when his high school girl-friend, long since moved away and on with her life, had gotten mar-ried to some lawyer in St. Louis. I don't think it was a broken heart over her that made Cal hit the bottle so much as it was the knowl-edge that the life he was living in Barren Springs—working for Land, helping me raise Junie, taking Mama groceries once in a while to keep her from starving—was the one he was most likely going to live forever. We'd never talked about it, though, because Cal would have never admitted that to anyone, probably not even to himself.

I pushed gently against his shoulder, said his name again, and he raised his head, fastened his bleary eyes to the right of me. "Eve?" he said, and I leaned backward, out of the range of his whiskey-fume breath. "What's going on?"

"You're drunk," I told him, trying to lay hands on my patience, my kindness. Because if anyone deserved a night of oblivion, it was Cal. It wasn't fair to always expect him to be the strong one. I won-dered how many hours he'd been putting in since Junie's death. Cal was the one who always worried about me, but who worried about him? Made sure he was eating and sleeping, gave him a hug even when he tried to shrug away? Told him everything would be okay? I made a vow to myself to do better by him when all this was over. Assuming I was still around to keep such a promise. "Come on," I said. "Let's get you home."

"No," he said when I gave his arm a tug. "Sit with me for a min-ute, Evie." He smiled at me. "Please."

I shot Keith a helpless look. "It's okay," he said. "I gotta go in the back and wash up some glasses, lock things up. I'll give you two a few."

"Thanks, Keith. We won't be long."

Cal squinted up at the clock behind the bar. "What time is it?"

"One thirty," I told him.

"Aw, shit," he muttered. "I'm sorry. Keith didn't need to call you. I'm fine."

I laughed. "Definitely not fine, cowboy. You can barely keep your eyes open and your ass on that stool."

Cal clutched the bar with both hands at my words, sat up a little straighter. "Have you seen the papers?" he asked me.

"What?" I shook my head. "What are you talking about? No."

He loosened one hand from the bar and reached inside his jacket, pulled out a folded-over newspaper and slapped it onto the bar. My own face blared up at me from the front page of the *Kansas City Star*, my skin pale, eyes wild, mouth a snarl. Caught midsentence at the press conference. Nobody who looked at that photo would care about the person who killed my daughter. I was the monster now.

"This one's from a few days ago. Look familiar?" Cal asked, tapping the photo. "Because if I didn't know better, I'd say that was Mama. Spitting image."

He wasn't wrong. Younger, less used up, maybe. But my mama all the same. "I already said I shouldn't have done it. What more do you want from me?" I turned the paper over so I didn't have to see. "Is that what caused this? Seeing me splashed all over the front page looking like a psycho? As far as I'm concerned, you should be thanking me."

Cal squinted, processing my words. "How you figure that?" he asked finally.

"Thanks to me and my total fuckup at that stupid press conference, all those reporters are gone. Chasing more interesting stories." I said it flippantly, but inside it stung. I didn't like having them here, following me around, ambushing me with their nosy questions. But having them gone meant they no longer cared, the wider world forgetting Junie already. Tragedy's attention span was short to begin with. Add in a white trash victim and an unsympathetic mother, and it shrank to almost nothing.

Cal scrubbed his face with one hand, the pulling motion making his skin sag, a little preview of his future. "You ever think we're still stuck in that trailer with Mama?" He didn't wait for me to answer, to point out he'd taken a conversational U-turn I could hardly keep up with or make sense of. "'Cause I do. Sometimes I'd swear all this is a dream and we're still kids who never got away." He shook his head, drained the dregs of his whiskey before I could stop him, set the glass down with a clank. "When I think back to growing up, to being around Mama, you know what always sticks out the most? That time we were out playing, building a fort or some shit. I'm guessing we were about five and six. Thereabouts, anyway. It was winter, cold, and I had a new hat and mittens. New to me anyway. Who the hell knows where Mama got them. Knowing her, she stole them from some other kid. Anyway, we were out in the woods and that little shit Randall . . . What was his last name? You remember?"

"Goff," I said. Remembered the whole story and wished I didn't have to hear it. But Cal was on a roll now, liquor loosening his tongue. "He was always a pain in the ass."

Cal nodded in agreement. "He took that hat right off my head. Snatched it and dared me to do anything about it. And when we got home, Mama took one look at me and asked where the hat was. Woman never cared what the hell we got up to, could be passed out drunk ninety-nine out of a hundred times we walked through the door, but that one time she had to be paying attention."

I remembered, too, how my stomach had sunk when she'd asked the question. There'd been a quick glance between Cal and me, followed by the inability to come up with a lie fast enough to ward her off. Her bony hand gripping Cal's arm, whipping him around to face her while I melted away into the wall, praying for invisibility.

"God, I'll never forget the look on her face when I told her. The total disgust and disappointment." His voice morphed into our mama's nastiest drawl, and my skin rippled. "'You let somebody take what's yours? You walk back in here still standing upright? Still breathing while that little asshole is out there wearing your hat? What's the matter with you, boy? Nobody takes something of yours, not if you're alive to stop them.'"

The real lesson had started after the tongue-lashing, when she'd grabbed the mittens off Cal's tiny hands, told him to get them back, not to let her have them. What kind of weak, pathetic pussy was he to let her take his mittens? It had ended only when she'd beaten him to a pulp, thrown the mittens in his busted-up face. Crouched down in front of me where I cowered in the corner and slapped me hard. "Never let anybody take something from you. You hear me? You get it back or you die trying." One thing you could say about our mama: Her lessons stuck. I've never forgotten a one.

Cal pulled his wallet and his badge from his back pocket, threw some twenties on the bar. "You know, she's the reason I became a cop," he said, rubbing his fingers over his badge. "Mama."

"Because you were hoping that someday you'd get to arrest her sorry ass?"

Cal smiled, but it didn't touch his eyes. "You and I both know, she'd kill me with her bare hands before she let me fasten cuffs on her wrists. Nah, I did it because I wanted to go a different way. Prove to her, and myself, that she doesn't know everything about the world. That not everything is ugly. Not everyone is bad. That I could still do some good." He heaved himself off his stool, shrugged away from my hand when I tried to steady him. His laugh was like a cracked branch as he staggered toward the door. "Turns out it was a colossal waste of my time. Because that old bitch was right. About all of it."

"What happened to Junie wasn't your fault," I said to his retreating back. Because even if he wasn't saying it, I knew what this bender was really about.

Cal stopped, looked at me over his shoulder, gaze skating from me to the newspaper he'd left on the bar and back again. "I wasn't talking about Junie," he said. "I was talking about you and me, Eve. Turning out exactly how Mama raised us."

SEVENTEEN

I was well aware that showing up at Jimmy Ray's compound with-out an express invitation was something akin to suicide. But I had to find a way to speak to Matt alone, without the protective cover of the strip club, where he could have me tossed out or simply walk away. I'd spent the last couple of days trying to come up with alter-native ideas, but I needed to catch him off guard if I had any hope of getting him to talk. I did think about calling Land, letting him know what I'd discovered. But I had a feeling the cops were already privy to my information and that there was a less-than-nothing chance they'd been able to get Matt to say a single word. I had seri-ous doubts I could get him to talk, either. Would probably leave this encounter with a black eye or some broken fingers, if I was lucky. But I had to try.

I wasn't so far gone, though, that I went in blind, with no hope of rescue if things went completely sideways. Cal sounded harried and exhausted when he answered the phone. We hadn't talked since I'd driven him home from the bar two nights ago. I'd been waiting for him to contact me first. I wanted to give him a chance to decide how he'd play it, suspecting he'd prefer to pretend his moment of weakness had never happened. He wouldn't want to be reminded that he'd needed me for a change. Or that memories of Mama still had such a hold on him after all these years.

"Hey," I said, pinning the phone between my ear and shoulder. I rolled up my car window as I drove, silencing the roaring wind.

"Hey," Cal said. "Everything okay?" He sounded a little surprised, and I realized I never called him anymore. Before Junie died, I'd talked to him at least twice a day, to shoot the shit, check in. But that lifelong routine had stopped along with my daughter's beating heart. Truth was, I didn't have anything to say and didn't have the energy to pretend to care what anyone else said, either, unless they were telling me who'd killed my girl.

"Yeah, everything's fine," I lied, half my brain calculating how far I was from Jimmy Ray's versus how long it might take Cal to get where I was going. "But listen, I got a lead on the guy Izzy was fooling around with and—"

"Eve," Cal said, sharp and loud. "What are you doing?"

My teeth clattered together as my car jounced over the uneven ground toward Jimmy Ray's compound. It was starting to get dark, and I felt spotlighted and vulnerable, my headlights and choppy engine announcing my arrival. "Don't worry," I told Cal, his disbelieving gust of breath telling me how likely that was. "I'm fine. I won't do anything dumb." The lies were rolling off my tongue like water now. "I wanted you to know I'm out at Jimmy Ray's, in case anything happens."

"No," Cal said. "Turn around right now. Eve, I'm serious. Turn—"

I hung up on him, powered off my phone, and threw it onto the passenger seat. I figured I had thirty minutes, maybe, before Cal caught up to me. That would be enough time, because Matt was either going to talk or he wasn't.

Up ahead I could see the tiny guard station Jimmy Ray had built out of plywood and scrap metal. It stood on the edge of his property, and there was no way to drive down his lane without passing it. A spotlight shone from its lopsided roof, and the whole jury-rigged look of it would have been funny if not for the armed redneck I knew waited inside.

But when I pulled to a stop next to the guard station, it was empty. I'd been practicing my speech in my head, the collection of words I'd hoped would get me past this barricade, and I wasn't quite sure what to do with myself now that they weren't needed. The thick metal chain that usually barred entrance to Jimmy Ray's compound when the guard station was unmanned lay coiled in the brush. The apparent ease of my entry left a hissing snake of worry in my gut. I'd never known Jimmy Ray to be careless with security. But a trap didn't seem like his style, either. Jimmy Ray wasn't sneaky. He didn't plot out ruses to get at you sideways. He came full throttle and right in your face. Maybe the guy manning the entrance had to take a leak and forgot about the chain. Maybe something at the compound required his urgent attention. Which might end up working in my favor. If everyone was distracted, that gave me more time with Matt.

I drove past the guard station, wincing a little as I remembered the few times I'd let Jimmy Ray talk me into bringing Junie out here. My worst moments as a mother rising up along with the shadows creeping out from the stands of trees lining the road. Back then, Matt lived in a trailer on the western edge of Jimmy Ray's property, and I was guessing that was still the case. Once Jimmy Ray's henchmen staked out a piece of land, they were reluctant to move. And if memory served, Matt's trailer might have been a broken-down tin can like my mama's, but he was close to the creek and had a view of the rolling hills out of his back windows.

The road curved, and I eased my car onto the shoulder, following a set of tracks I knew from memory, not from sight. Branches slapped against my windows, and I thanked God for the lack of recent rain. Last thing I needed was to get bogged down, stuck out here with no way to escape. Just when I thought maybe I'd turned too early, I saw the half-rotted cabin Jimmy Ray had shown me once. It was the original homestead of the family who had owned this land years ago. Overgrown and hidden. We'd had sex there, me pressed up against the moss-covered walls and Junie asleep out in the car. I knew there was a wide-open patch of ground to turn my car around on, leave it facing out for a fast getaway.

There was no subtle way to approach Jimmy Ray's compound in a car. He'd built it at the base of a hill. Even with your lights off, you crested that rise and it was all over. The only chance you had to approach undetected was on foot, and the farther you stayed from Jimmy Ray, the better your chances. If things went right, I could cut through the woods, talk to Matt, and be back out again before Jimmy Ray even knew I'd been here. It was in Matt's best interest to make sure that's how it went down, too. Jimmy Ray only liked the drama he created. He didn't want to deal with anyone else's bullshit. The faster Matt got me out of here, the better for both of us.

I grabbed a flashlight out of my glove compartment and set off through the brush. Kudzu grabbed at my ankles, and overhead I could hear bats wheeling in the darkening sky. Off to my left, something slinked through the underbrush, and I made my footfalls louder in response. But I wasn't afraid. I'd grown up in these woods, knew them as well as I knew my own heartbeat. Nothing out here would hurt me without a fair fight.

I slowed as the trees thinned out, lights glowing in the near distance. I could see an ever-present ring of trucks outside of Jimmy Ray's house, but it was too far away for me to see any movement, especially in the growing dark. Ahead and to my left was the path leading to Matt's trailer. There was no way to avoid leaving the cover of the trees and being exposed, at least for a few moments. I'd worn jeans and a black shirt, and hoped that anyone who might spot me would be far enough away to simply assume I was one of their own. Almost all Jimmy Ray's men had girlfriends or wives, sometimes both, living on the compound, so my presence might not seem out of place.

I hesitated, listening, but heard nothing but the wind through the tops of the trees, the distant hoot of a barn owl. The time to go was now, but still I waited. Not sure if it was fear stopping my feet or some remnant of my lizard brain warning me not to move yet. I counted slowly to one hundred and then did it again. Nothing. I took a deep breath and pushed out of the trees, walking quickly, eyes straight ahead, toward the path to Matt's trailer. The sense of exposure, of being easy pickings, made the hair on the back of my neck stand up, and I resisted the urge to run. I was halfway there when I heard the sound of a car engine from the direction of Jimmy Ray's house. My heart burst forward in my chest, like it was trying to beat my body to the safety of the path, and I glanced to my right, saw headlights cresting the hill and sweeping across the long grass in front of me.

There was nowhere for me to go. I couldn't make it back to the woods before the lights reached me, so I surged forward, tripping a little as I broke into a run, scrambling forward to where the path disappeared over a rise. I threw myself into the long grass and rolled, my shoulder snagging on something sharp as I slid to a stop.

I waited, breathing in harsh pants, listening for the sound of voices or car doors opening. Jimmy Ray would have a field day with me. He'd make my broken wrist seem like amateur hour. But the car didn't stop, kept moving down the road and away from me. I lay there for a moment longer, pressing against the wound in my shoulder and watching my fingers come away red.

"Shit," I muttered, pushing myself up. A weird kind of embarrassment flooded me. What was I doing here, pretending to be some kind of badass avenger? What would Junie say if she could see me right now? Somehow I thought her reaction might be more eye roll than encouragement. But I'd come this far, could see the light glowing from the windows of Matt's trailer in the distance.

I trudged down the hill, feet sliding a little on the matted grass. Nobody out here locked their doors. I could barge in, catch him unawares. But everybody out here kept a loaded gun at the ready, too. And total surprise might end with a bullet in my belly. I decided knocking was probably the smartest way to go. Somehow I didn't think he'd refuse me entry. If nothing else, curiosity would probably get the best of him, like it did with most people.

I was still fifty yards away when I heard the twang of a country song from his windows. A few steps closer and I smelled the remnants of his dinner on the wind. Grilled meat and barbecue sauce. Another five yards and a strange whooshing noise stopped me in my tracks. Not the wind. I tried to place it, stomach plummeting as my brain clicked—the sucking noise a stove makes when you fire up the pilot light. And then the whole world exploded.

EIGHTEEN

I came to on the ground, stars above me, fire roaring in front of me, the sound of shouting in the distance. Everything was muffled, though, as if my head was encased in thick cotton. I rolled onto my side, and the world spun off its axis, bile rising in my throat. I lowered my head slowly until my forehead touched the grass, breathed in through my nose and out through my mouth until my stomach eased back down to its rightful position.

It took me a minute to remember where I was, what had happened. I pushed myself up onto my knees, one hand starfished on the ground for balance, and looked at the spot where Matt's trailer had been. All that was left of it were a few burning hunks of metal, pieces scattered across the ground, fire burning along the tree line on the other side of the clearing.

"What the fuck?" I said, my voice a hoarse croak.

I knew I needed to get back to my car, get out of here, but I couldn't seem to make my body follow the commands of my brain. From behind me, I heard the sound of running, and even as I stumbled to my feet, I knew I wasn't going to be able to outpace whoever it was. A man scrambled down the path toward me, slipping a little on the grass, and I steeled myself for what would come next. It was bad enough to trespass on Jimmy Ray's land. It was another thing entirely to be there when one of his men got blown to shit.

I squinted against the smoke blowing into my eyes, relief flooding me when I realized it was Cal coming toward me, not Jimmy Ray. Cal grabbed me as I stumbled forward, holding me up when my legs wanted to buckle.

"Eve," he practically shouted. "Jesus Christ. What the fuck is going on? What happened?"

I shook my head. "I don't know. I came to talk to him and . . ." I threw my arm out. "And it exploded. I never even saw him."

Cal looked over his shoulder. "You need to go," he said. "Before Jimmy Ray gets here." He gave me shove. "Go!"

"But—"

He shoved me again, harder this time. "For once in your life, Eve, don't argue with me! Go! *Now!*"

I stumbled away from him, legs jerking along about a half second behind my brain's instructions. Behind me I could hear Cal on his police radio calling in the explosion, asking for backup and an ambulance, although it was too late for Matt, or what was left of him. I'd cleared the edge of the woods when a pickup truck crested the rise. I stopped, hidden behind the trunk of a tree, and watched a half dozen of Jimmy Ray's men tumble out, shouting and racing toward Cal.

Part of me wanted to stay and make sure he would be okay, that Jimmy Ray and his men wouldn't take their anger out on him. But

I had to assume Cal's badge would protect him, at least until backup arrived. And he was right: I needed to get out of here. The longer I lingered, the greater the chance someone was going to find me.

I didn't really remember the rest of the walk back to the car, tripping over tree roots and stumbling in the dark. My hands were shaking so hard it took me three tries to get the key in the ignition, jaw clacking as I drove too fast out of the compound in a race to beat the cops I knew were on their way. When I got back onto the main road, I passed two of them, lights and sirens screaming as they headed toward Jimmy Ray's. I watched their taillights in my rearview mirror until they were out of sight, half expecting to see them turn around and come after me instead. My hands didn't unclench and my jaw didn't loosen until I'd pulled into a spot in my apartment complex. When I finally unwound myself from the driver's seat, my whole body felt like it had taken one of Jimmy Ray's beatings, and I walked hunched over and limping to my front door.

I locked myself in the bathroom and peeled out of my clothes, wincing as my shirt stuck to the gash on my shoulder. My face was streaked with soot, and I had a bruise starting on my left cheekbone, probably from where I hit the ground after the explosion. I held the edges of the porcelain sink to stop my hands from shaking, tried to wrap my brain around the last hour. Matt's trailer blowing up just as I was coming to talk to him made no sense to me. If Matt had been the one to kill Izzy and Junie, then why would he blow himself up? Remorse didn't seem like it would be a big concern to someone like Matt. Unlike Jimmy Ray himself, Matt, I suspected, didn't live by any kind of code. Killing two preteen girls probably wouldn't cost him a single second of sleep. And if he hadn't killed them, then why would the killer care if I talked to Matt? If anything, that would give the police someone else to focus on. Matt alive and having to explain his relationship with Izzy could only be a good thing for the killer. All eyes focused in the wrong direction.

Something was nagging at me, some tidbit of information that floated out of my reach whenever my brain tried to clamp down on it. But my entire body hurt, my brain most of all, and I knew the harder I pushed, the more elusive it would be. I stood in the shower for a long time, until the water washing over my shoulder turned from red to pink to crystal clear. So long the hot water gave out to a lukewarm spray. And still the thought wouldn't crystalize. Maybe a decent night's sleep would send whatever it was to the surface. Or maybe it was nothing at all.

I wrapped myself in a towel, double-checked the gash in my shoulder to make sure the bleeding had slowed before I covered it with a patch of gauze and a couple of Band-Aids, and then stepped out into the hallway. A floorboard creaked to my left, and as I turned my head, something heavy hit me from the side, slammed me back into the wall, my head smacking against the doorjamb. A hand around my throat, fingers calloused and rough.

"What did you do?" Jimmy Ray said, breath hot in my face. "You stupid bitch."

He expected me to cower, to plead, to placate. Because that was how this worked between us. Him winding tighter and tighter while I frantically tried to keep him calm, keep him contained, not wanting Junie to witness something that would scar her forever. But the world was a different place now, without my daughter in it. And I was a different woman.

I brought my knee up fast and hard, caught him right in the nuts because he wasn't expecting it, hadn't even thought to protect himself. Not from me. He let go of my neck, bent in half like someone had cut his strings, and fell to his knees. I shoved away from him, turned to run, and got two steps before his hand closed over my ankle and yanked. I hit the floor hard, landing on my hip, scrabbling for something to grab. My free leg shot out, foot slamming into his nose with an audible crunch, and he released my ankle, flopped onto his back, and cupped both hands over his face.

"Jesus Christ," he moaned. "What'd you do that for?" Said with the plaintive whine of bullies the world over, those who can dish it out but have never learned how to take it.

I used the wall for balance and pushed myself to standing. I yanked my towel off the floor and wrapped it around myself again. "Because you deserved it," I told him.

Surprisingly, he didn't argue with me. All the fight seemed to have gone out of him with that one kick, his nose sitting sideways on his face. I wondered if that was all it would have taken, years ago, to end things between us. No long drawn-out fights where it was my face bloodied and bruised, no blow job in Land's car to make Jimmy Ray finally disappear. It might have worked. Or I might have ended up dead and dumped in the woods somewhere, Junie left to be raised by Cal or, God forbid, my mama. Second-guessing the past wasn't going to do me any good. All I knew for sure was tonight, this moment.

I watched, warily, as Jimmy Ray shoved himself up to sitting, leaned his back against the wall. "Can I get a towel?" he asked.

I went into the kitchen, gathered some ice in a dish towel, and brought it back to him. He wiped the blood off his face and then tipped his head back, pressed the ice pack to his nose with a groan. "Damn, girl," he said. "You got me good."

I slid down the wall and sat beside him, legs out in front of me and crossed at the ankle in deference to the towel I was still wearing. "I didn't blow up Matt's trailer."

Jimmy Ray glanced at me. "Yeah, I figured that was a long shot."

"But you thought you'd break into my apartment and strangle me anyway?"

"I was pissed," Jimmy Ray said with a shrug. "Got cops crawling all over my place. Besides, if I really wanted you dead, you'd be dead. Your mama be damned."

I turned to look at him. "What's my mama got to do with it?"

"Back when we was together, your mama used to give me what for. Told me if I ever went too far, she'd use my dick as fish bait."

I stared at him, momentarily speechless. Sure, when I was a kid, Mama had lit into anyone who'd wronged me. But as an adult, I thought she'd stopped caring even that much. Once, when she'd seen one of the black eyes Jimmy Ray had given me, she'd told me I'd gotten myself into that mess and I had to get strong enough to find my way back out. It had never occurred to me that she'd given Jimmy Ray any kind of warning.

"What?" Jimmy Ray said, amused. "Why'd you think that broken wrist is the worst you ever got? Hell, I was a little worried about that one, to be honest. Thought maybe my pecker was a goner."

"Then I guess it's a good thing for you that strangling me didn't work out."

Jimmy Ray reached over and grabbed my hand, squeezed it just this side of pain. "I'm not fucking around, Eve," he said. "I got some affection for ya. God knows why because you've been a thorn in my side more often than not. But that affection goes only so far." He dropped my hand, gestured to his face. "You pull something like this again? Or something like what happened out at my place tonight? Your brother'll be fishing bits of you out of the river. Tiny bits. And your mama can go fuck herself." He held my gaze. "You understand?"

"Yes," I said, because I did. I'd used up all my chips with Jimmy Ray. And he wasn't the kind of guy to give you a loan. "I honestly don't know what happened out there tonight. I wanted to talk to Matt, that's all. He was messing around with Junie's friend Izzy."

"So you figured you'd sneak onto my land?" Jimmy Ray shook his head. "For someone who didn't want to be strangled, you got some kind of death wish, Eve."

I shrugged. "Sounds about right." I straightened the towel across my lap. "You got any theories about Matt?"

"I got no fucking idea," Jimmy Ray said. But the slight pause before he answered, the hiccups between his words, made me think he probably had at least a sneaking suspicion. "He sometimes cooked up meth in there, I know. We've moved on to heroin. Bigger market these days." He spoke about his drug trade like he talked about the weather or what he'd had for dinner. Something ordinary, a given. "But Matt liked meth, for himself. Maybe he got sloppy. Blew himself to bits. He always was kind of a dumb fucker."

"Maybe," I said. "Or maybe somebody helped him along."

Jimmy Ray looked at me again. I could feel his dark eyes burning into the side of my face. "Why? What's the benefit in Matt being dead?"

"I don't know. Maybe he knew something about what happened to Junie and Izzy. Maybe someone didn't want him talking."

Jimmy Ray flicked my leg with one hand. "Hate to break it to you, sweetheart, but Matt wasn't never gonna talk to you. And I seriously doubt he had any information about the murders anyway. That guy barely knew his ass from a hole in the ground."

My head thunked back against the wall. "I have no idea then. About anything." I paused, closed my eyes. "I keep trying to make sense of it. Why they died. What happened. What the point of it was."

"Waste of your time, Eve. Like pissing into the wind. Trying to answer that question, the why of a thing like that'll drive you round the bend. The why don't matter."

"Then what does?"

"The who. The person who held the knife. That's the only thing that really matters."

It didn't escape me, how weird this conversation was. Jimmy Ray and I sitting here nursing our wounds and shooting the shit like we were old friends. Hell, maybe that's what he thought we were. It reminded me, in the worst kind of way, of me and my mama. No matter how often I thought I was finally rid of her, somehow we always seemed to end up sitting across from each other again. Both she and Jimmy Ray had some kind of staying power, I'd give them that. "I still feel like you know more than you're telling me," I said, gathering my wet hair into a knot on top of my head.

"Nah," Jimmy Ray said, stood up and held out his hand. He hauled me to my feet. "I know as much as you do."

"What does that mean, exactly?" I ducked my head to try and catch his eyes, his face averted from mine. Jimmy Ray who used eye contact as a kind of weapon, for seduction, for intimidation. He was a man who knew the power of his gaze. I knew it meant something that he wouldn't look at me now.

He turned away from me, limping a little from the knee to the groin earlier. Which, I admit, gave me a twinge of satisfaction. "You know what I always liked best about you?"

I thought back to the compliments he'd given me over the years. "My legs?"

He did look at me then, over his shoulder, eyes sliding from my hips to my bare ankles. "Always did love your legs. They still look damn good." He smirked. "They'd look even better wrapped around my waist."

I was suddenly aware of my nakedness, how one quick yank would send my towel flying. A surge of excitement followed the thought, chased immediately by a flush of shame. What was wrong with me that a man like Jimmy Ray made my body react so easily, heat in my belly and wetness between my legs with only a few words? Especially when that same body knew the pain he could inflict? I took a step backward, away from him.

"If not my legs, then what?" I tried to keep my voice brisk and businesslike, but I heard the huskiness in my tone. Jimmy Ray heard it, too, if the way his smirk had turned into a full-on grin was any indication.

He threw me a wink to let me know I wasn't getting away with anything, and then his expression turned serious. "I liked how smart you are. All the other girls I've dated"—he tapped his temple—"not much in the way of candlepower."

"I thought you liked it that way," I said. "Less chance they'll argue with you."

Jimmy Ray's hand swiped through the air, swatting away my words. "Pay attention to what I'm saying. You're smart, Eve. You've got stuff going on upstairs. It made you a pain in the ass to deal with a lot of the time, but you were never boring. I'll give you that."

I thought Jimmy Ray's attempt at a compliment was probably bullshit, had more than a sneaking suspicion that he'd called me a dumb-ass cunt a hundred times behind my back. I tightened my hands on the top of my towel. "Why are you telling me this?"

"Because it's all right there." He poked his temple again. "You can figure this out."

"What if I'm not as smart as you think?"

"You are," Jimmy Ray said. "But maybe you're focusing on the wrong things."

"You mean Matt?"

"I mean there's only a few reasons people kill each other." He ticked them off on his fingers. "Sex, money, or pure rage."

I was getting frustrated now, unsure whether he actually knew anything or if he was screwing with me. "Which one was it, if you know so much?"

"I'm not saying I *know* anything," Jimmy Ray said. "I'm saying you may be going down the wrong path, is all." Which sounded at least partly self-serving to me. Jimmy Ray wanted me out of his business and away from his compound. Matt was out of the picture, and now I needed to follow his lead.

"Maybe you blew up Matt yourself to keep me from talking to him."

Jimmy Ray laughed. "Girl, you've been watching too many movies. I'm gonna go to all the trouble of setting up an explosion when I can walk up to the man and shoot him? A gun's a lot quieter and doesn't bring a bunch of cops down on my head." He opened my front door. "Besides, what do I give a shit if Matt talks to you? I already told you I had nothing to do with your girl dying." He paused in the half-open doorway. "From what I hear, there wasn't any sex involved in the killings. And it doesn't sound like rage, either. Not the way they were laid out all nice and neat. What's that leave?" He looked at me over his shoulder as he closed the door, the pity in his eyes so completely foreign I wondered if even he knew it was there. "Follow the money, Eve. Follow the money."

NINETEEN

Follow the money? What the fuck was that supposed to mean? We didn't have any money. Not me, not Junie, not Cal or my mama, either. No one in my family had ever had two nickels to rub together. That left Izzy. Her family definitely had more money, but they weren't anywhere close to loaded. Hell, somewhere else they'd probably barely be considered middle class. And I somehow couldn't picture Izzy involved in some grand scheme involving loads of dough. She was twelve, for God's sake. More interested in nail polish, and texting, and nursing inappropriate crushes on idiots like Matt. But maybe there was something I couldn't see because I wasn't close enough. Something hidden within a family I only knew from the outside edges.

I'd managed to throw on some clothes and put my hair in a

ponytail when Cal showed up, sweaty and smelling of smoke, his uniform torn at the sleeve and his shoes covered in ash. He wasn't quite as furious as Jimmy Ray had been earlier, but he was close.

"What the hell, Eve," he said, pacing my living room floor. Every step left tiny black soot marks on the worn-out carpet. "What were you doing out there? You could have gotten beat to hell or killed! And that's before Matt's place blew all to shit." He raked a hand through his hair, leaving the dirty strands standing on end.

"I already told you on the phone," I said. "The guy messing around with Izzy. It was Matt."

"So what?" Cal yelled. "Since when is it your job to go out there half-cocked? That's what the cops are for!"

"Then why hadn't you talked to him yet?" I yelled back. "Now he's dead and it's too goddamn late."

Cal stopped pacing and turned to face me where I was curled up in the corner the sofa. "What makes you think we haven't talked to him?"

That stopped me, what I was going to say next stumbling on the end of my tongue. "Why didn't you say that when I called?"

"Because you hung up on me and went to confront him on your own like a nutcase!"

Cal and I hadn't talked to each other like this in years. This was how we always used to interact when we were younger. Me, belligerent and impulsive and borderline self-destructive. And Cal constantly trying to undo the damage I'd done, trying to get me to see the error of my ways, frustration boiling over when I didn't listen. But with Junie's arrival our dynamic had shifted. Having a child made me vulnerable in a way I'd never felt before. Growing up, I hadn't cared what happened to me. But Junie needed me. So I took Cal's protection, his concerns, and cocooned both Junie and myself inside them like Bubble Wrap. I wondered if the other night, Cal drunk in the bar, slurring his words and speaking truths about our childhood, had knocked something loose between us. Grief spilling over and turning us back into the past versions of ourselves.

"What did he say when you asked him about Izzy?"

Cal sank down onto the couch next to me and threw his head back, closed his eyes. "Not much. He tried denying it at first, but we kept pressing him."

"You and Land?"

"Mmm-hmm. Eventually he said they'd been flirting a little bit, but that it hadn't progressed beyond the talking stage."

I shifted to look at him. "You believe that?"

Cal opened his eyes. "No. But just because he was screwing around with her doesn't mean he killed her."

"What did you think, though, when you talked to him?"

Cal sighed. "Who the hell knows with a guy like that? He lied as easy as breathing. Pretty much every word out of his mouth was designed to cover his own ass." He took a step closer to me. "We got the text messages off Izzy's phone."

"What? When? What did they say?"

"Slow down," Cal said. "The only one that stood out came the day they died. Whoever it was texted her that morning. Told her to meet him at the park. Neither one of them mentioned Junie being there." He gave a helpless shrug. "I'm assuming it's a he, for now."

"It was someone Izzy knew?" I asked. It should have been a relief. The line between a killer and his victims running straight through the Logans' daughter and not mine. But I didn't trust the feeling, my gut still churning, telling me Junie was a part of what happened, somehow.

"Apparently."

"Did the text say anything about money?"

Cal's brow furrowed. "Money? Like blackmail? What do you mean?"

I stood up, gathered a few dirty glasses from the coffee table. "I don't know what I mean." I walked toward the kitchen and set the glasses in the sink. "Someone mentioned maybe money was at the root of all this." I concentrated on running some water, squirting a little dish soap.

"Who is *someone?*" Cal called, and I regretted saying anything because as soon as Jimmy Ray's name left my lips, all rational conversation was going to end. "Who, Evie?" Cal asked again, getting up and looming in the doorway to the kitchen. When I didn't answer, Cal smacked a hand against the doorjamb. "It was fucking Jimmy Ray, wasn't it? That piece of shit. When did you talk to him?"

"He was here tonight, earlier."

All the bluster went out of Cal, and he stepped closer, put a gentle hand on my arm. "Did he hurt you?"

I shrugged, looked away. "Not as much as he wanted to. I think I broke his nose."

A long low whistle from Cal. "Holy shit, Eve. Good for you."

I laughed, a short exhale. "Between the two of us, we're giving Jimmy Ray's face a whole new look."

Cal grin lasted only a moment before it dropped away and something more serious took its place. "You know he's probably screwing with you, right? Winding you up?"

"Why would he do that?" I asked, but it was a stupid question. Jimmy Ray loved playing with people, loved having the upper hand and watching everyone dance while he pulled the strings.

"Because he can," Cal said, exasperated. "Because it's fun. Because he likes feeling powerful. Do you need me to go on?"

I left the dirty dishes soaking in the sink and grabbed a towel from the counter to dry my hands. "You're saying he's totally off base, money had nothing to do with it?"

"I'm not saying that. Up until now, we haven't found that connection, but that doesn't mean it's not there. But if it is, it would be a lucky guess on Jimmy Ray's part. He doesn't know shit about what happened, Evie. He's trying to get inside your head."

What Cal was saying made perfect, logical sense. It was Jimmy Ray's modus operandi from way back. But still, I couldn't quite let the idea go. I kept thinking of Jimmy Ray's face when he'd spoken to me, the swift flash of tenderness I almost hadn't recognized because it was so unexpected. The light in his eyes that burned with something close to truth.

. . .

Grief hadn't put a damper on Jenny Logan's green thumb. The flower pots lining her front steps were a riot of early spring colors: Pink, white, and yellow burst forth, tiny faces tipped to the sun. I wondered if looking at the flowers made her pain more bearable, hope sealing up some of the cracks in her heart. Personally, I wanted to rip the flowers out of the dirt and grind them to dust under my heels. But I figured that might get our conversation off on the wrong foot.

If Jenny was surprised to find me on her front porch, she didn't show it. She ushered me in with a gesturing hand and a promise of coffee. I saw her eyes flit to the pale purple bruises Jimmy Ray had left near my collarbone, but her good manners stopped her from asking any embarrassing questions. Or maybe she couldn't bring herself to care.

We settled at her small kitchen table, tucked next to a window that overlooked her backyard. It was wilder back there, weeds and crabgrass edging out her half-hearted attempts at control. I guess she only worried about the front yard, the place everyone could see. The whole house was shabbier than I would have expected. The rooms I'd passed were cramped and claustrophobic under too-low ceilings, the light from outside somehow failing to penetrate the dim interior. Maybe it had always been this way, or maybe the house was in mourning, too. There were still three chairs at the kitchen table, and I imagined Izzy's empty seat howling at them during every meal.

Jenny seemed content for the two of us to sip our coffee, pick at the edges of coffee cake slices she'd set out on a plate. She didn't seem in any hurry to know why I was there. Made no attempt at small talk or pleasantries. I was beginning to realize that Jenny Logan had one face she showed the world—put-together, sweet, unfailingly polite—and another for behind closed doors. This private Jenny was less concerned with what people thought. I wondered what this Jenny would have done if she'd found out that Junie was Zach's daughter.

I set down my coffee mug, cleared my throat to catch her attention. "I've been thinking about motive," I told her.

"Motive?" She said the word like she'd never heard it before.

"Yeah, there are only a handful of reasons why people commit murder." I realized I was parroting Jimmy Ray and shut my mouth with a click of my jaw.

"People commit murder because they're evil," Jenny said, pushing the plate of coffee cake away like it had offended her.

"That's what they are," I agreed, "but that's not why they do it. There's a reason." I paused. "Are you and Zach having money problems or anything?"

Jenny cocked her head. She didn't look angry, only confused.

"No. We could always use more, but who couldn't?" She ran her gaze around her kitchen, the old appliances, the out-of-date tile. "People forget Zach only works at the dealership. We don't own it. And Zach's got a lot of great qualities, but schmoozy salesman isn't one of them. What's money got to do with anything?"

"Someone suggested to me that money might be at the root of this."

"You think someone killed them over *money*?" Jenny's head wagged side to side in denial.

"I don't think anything. I'm just asking the question. For the record, my money problems are the same as they've always been. Not enough of it. But I don't owe anyone, other than occasionally the electric company." I gave a weak smile that Jenny didn't return.

"What about your mother?" she asked after a moment.

My hand froze, the piece of coffee cake I was worrying slipping between my fingers. "What about her?"

Jenny shifted in her chair, but she kept her eyes on me, not looking away the way most people did when my mama was the subject of conversation. "Come on, Eve," she said. "Everyone in town knows about your mama. The crowd she runs with. The kind of stuff she's mixed up in. If this *was* over money, it stands to reason that maybe it involves her."

"She didn't even know Junie," I shot back. "Someone hurting Junie wouldn't matter to my mama."

Jenny stopped fidgeting, hand grasping hard around her coffee mug. "We both know that's not true. There's two basic facts about your mama that are never in dispute: She runs with a rough crowd, and you don't mess with her family. *Any* of her family. If someone wanted to teach her a lesson, I imagine that's where they'd start."

My heart thundered in my chest. I wanted to lash out with

self-righteousness, scoff at her claims and force an apology. But not a single false word had left her lips. Hadn't I known, deep down, that this was always going to come back to me, to my family? I'd tried to pretend like Izzy might be the key, but I knew she wasn't. It was Junie. It was me.

But I couldn't roll over and take it. Because admitting it out loud was a step too far. It was one thing for me to know; it was another to lay myself bare to Jenny Logan. "What about Izzy and the older guy she was seeing?" I heard myself ask, hating how easily the question left my mouth. Jenny's head snapped back like I'd slapped her, her eyes wide with surprise. But not shock. She'd known about Izzy, I realized, but not that I was in on the secret, too. "When did you find out?" I asked.

"When Land told me. A few days ago." She shook her head. "Not before that."

"You'd never seen her with Matt?"

"No. I would have put a stop to it if I'd known." Spoken like a woman who couldn't imagine a defiant, sneaky daughter. Who knew nothing of the myriad ways girls will find to circumvent their parents' rules: broken window screens and bedsheet ladders, secret notes and messages passed from friends, *yes ma'ams* followed just as quickly by a rolled eye and a hidden smirk.

"I would have liked to hear what Matt had to say about it. See his face while I asked him some questions."

Jenny's mouth twisted, her eyes going distant and hard. "Yeah, well, he's dead. He won't be saying much of anything anymore."

I stared at her across the table, and she stared back. She didn't look like polished, polite Jenny Logan anymore. She looked like a mother whose daughter had been wronged—the scariest creature in the world. After the murders, I'd made the easy assumption that her tears meant weakness, but I was learning that nothing about Jenny Logan was weak. I heard again the eerie, whooshing silence the moment before Matt's trailer exploded. Heat and light and sound slamming in to me, bowling me over like a runway truck. Did Jenny Logan have it in her to light that match, flip that switch? Looking at her face right now, I didn't doubt it for a second. For the first time, I felt a kinship with her. Suffering the same loss hadn't bonded us, but maybe fury would.

I opened my mouth to say something, some acknowledgment of what I read in her eyes, but as I began to speak, her face cleared, rearranging itself back into bland, agreeable Jenny Logan. "There you are," she said, looking at something over my shoulder. "Coffee?"

I turned in my chair, already knowing who I would see and dreading it. Zach stood in the doorway, his plaid shirt half unbuttoned, white T-shirt peeking out. He wore jeans and his feet were bare, hair still damp from the shower. My stomach slid downward at the sight of him, remembering the feel of his skin against mine. His eyes shifted from his wife to me, lingered until I wanted to cross the room and slap him, force him to turn his head in a different direction. I shifted away instead, turned my gaze back to my own coffee cup.

"Hey there," Zach said, his voice moving closer. "What did I miss down here?"

Jenny was bustling away at the counter, pouring coffee and adding a splash of milk, the well-practiced movements of a wife who no longer has to think about what her husband might like. His wants as ingrained as her own. "Nothing," she said. "Eve wanted to see how I'm doing." She turned, held out the mug to Zach.

I slid my chair back, and it screeched against the floor. "I should get out of your hair. Thanks for the coffee."

"I'll walk you out," Zach said.

"No, finish your coffee, I'm fine." I cut across the kitchen toward the front hall, and Zach drifted along in my wake. "What are you doing?" I whispered to him, jerking my arm away when he put a hand on my elbow.

"You didn't come here to see Jenny," he said, voice pitched as low as mine.

I laughed, short and sharp, turned to face him. "Yeah, I did, actually."

His hand found my collarbone, smoothed hair back over my shoulder, fingers skimming my bruises. His brow furrowed. "What happened here?"

"Nothing. I'm fine."

His fingers lingered, raising goose bumps on my skin. "I think about you. All the time."

I slapped at his hand. "Are you insane? We've gone more than a decade without saying ten words to each other, and suddenly I'm all you think about? How stupid do you think I am?"

"Not stupid at all," Zach said, face serious. "And it's not sudden." That's what made it almost impossible to stay mad at him, to even *be* mad at him. His earnestness, his absolute belief in whatever it was he was telling you. You might know it was bullshit, but Zach never did. Which in some ways made him even worse than Jimmy Ray. At least with Jimmy Ray what you saw was always what you got.

I wrenched open the front door, shot Zach a look over my shoulder. "Stop it," I said, as loud as I dared. "It was sex. And it was good. But it didn't mean anything. Get back in that kitchen and have coffee with your wife. I am *not* what you want. Trust me." Even now, sparing his feelings. The way women are taught to behave.

Making it about what was good for him instead of what was bad for me.

"What do *you* want?" Zach asked, like he actually thought the answer might be him. It almost made me pity him for being such a child. He still didn't understand that what this might have been once upon a time made no difference anymore. One-night stand lust, potential true love, lifelong friendship. All the possibilities ceased to matter the moment Junie died.

"I want to wake up tomorrow and have a daughter again. Or I want to wake up the day I met you and call in sick to the diner. Rewrite history." I shrugged. "I want this pain to go away. Can you make that happen?"

Zach shook his head, his eyes ancient. "No."

I stepped out onto the porch. "Then grow up, because you don't have anything I need."

TWENTY

I'd visited my mama's trailer more since Junie's death than I had in the entire time she'd been alive. It scared me how familiar it all felt, how I slipped back into it like I'd never managed to claw my way out. It fed into my horrified suspicion that this was where I was always destined to end up. That my time as my daughter's mother had been only a momentary blip, a brief respite from my true nature. That what I really was, and always had been, was my mother's daughter.

The rusted black pickup was still parked in my mama's yard, but this time I got the dubious pleasure of meeting the man who drove it. Or at least I assumed the guy passed out on my mama's ripped faux-leather sofa was the owner. One homemade-tattoo-covered arm thrown over his face, a sliver of hairy beer belly winking at me where his T-shirt failed to meet the waistband of his dirty jeans. He was so exactly my mama's type she might as well have picked him out of a catalog.

He barely stirred when I let myself in, tattered screen door slamming behind me. "Mama?" I called. "You in here?" Too keyed up to be careful, forgetting all the protocols in place to keep things on an even keel. Don't scream, don't demand, don't surprise. My mama was like a rabid dog that way, one mistake in the approach and you were as good as dead.

"Jesus Christ, quiet the fuck down," my mama hissed from the direction of the kitchen. She came around from behind the fridge, a beer in one hand and a cigarette in the other. "Got half a mind to kick your ass," she said. "Barging in here like you own the place."

The thing that had been nagging at me, plucking my mind like a violin string over and over until it about drove me crazy, had come rushing in as I'd left the Logans' house this morning. The first time I'd let it go in what felt like forever, and suddenly there it was, my mind laying it out in front of me like a hog on a platter, ripe for the taking. I pointed at her, took two steps in her direction. "How did you know what Junie's walk was like?" I demanded.

My mama's brow wrinkled up. "What in the hell are you talking about?" She swirled her cigarette hand beside her head. "Has grief made you loony, or what?"

The man on the couch lowered his arm, squinted at me through bleary eyes. "Who the hell are you?" he said. "What's going on?"

"Shut up," I said without looking at him, kept my eyes glued on my mama. "In my house the other day, in my kitchen. You said you knew about Zach and me because he and Junie have the same walk."

My mama stubbed her cigarette out on the countertop, flicked it into the sink. "Yeah, so?"

"How'd you know? How do you know Junie's walk well enough

to recognize it in Zach? And don't give me some bullshit about seeing her from a distance. You've never been that close to her, not for
long enough to matter." I wanted those words to be the truth, *needed*
them to be, but I already suspected they weren't, long before my
mama opened her mouth and confirmed it.

"You got some nerve, coming into my home, accusing me." She
paused, took a swig from her beer. "What exactly is it you're accusing me of, anyway? Knowing how your daughter *walked?*" Her voice
turned high and full of fake panic. "Quick, someone call the cops. I
should be arrested. I'm a goddamn menace to society."

That's how you always knew my mama felt cornered, backed
against the wall by her own lies. She came out swinging, wild and
mean, and she didn't care who she took down in her wake.

I sank down into one of the wobbly chairs clustered around the
scarred kitchen table, leaned forward until my forehead almost
touched my knees. "You knew her," I said, more to myself than to
my mama. "You knew Junie." It was my worst nightmare come
true. Everything I'd tried to protect her from, insulate her against,
walking right up and making itself at home.

"I was her grandma."

I shot upward so fast tiny stars sparked in my vision. "I was her
mother. And I told you no. I told you to stay the fuck away from her!"
I slammed one hand down onto the table, wondered how bad a
price I might have to pay for the startled jump it caused my mama.
"Isn't that what you always said when we were growing up, to anyone who tried to interfere, stick their noses in our business trying
to help Cal and me? That you were our mama and you made the
rules?"

She stared at me, even and calm now. "I did say that."

"I always knew you were poison. And I'd made my peace with

that, with the part of me that comes from you. But you weren't supposed to touch her, none of your filth or your meanness or your awful decisions were ever going to get close to Junie." I paused, a horrible thought bubbling to the surface. "Are you the one who introduced Izzy to Matt? Is that how she met him?"

"I got no idea what you're talking about," my mama said, brow furrowed. "I never even met Izzy."

I believed her only because she wouldn't bother lying, not about something she'd consider as unimportant as bringing Matt into Izzy's orbit. I palmed tears off my cheek with the flat of my hand. I glanced around the trailer with blurry eyes, half-finished beer cans littering the counters, a scrum of suspicious white powder smeared at the other end of the table, the thick, hot smell of rotting garbage, the blare of idiotic voices from the television in the corner. Something like horror swelled in my chest. "Did Junie come here? Did you bring her *here*?"

"You ashamed of growing up poor?" my mama asked. "Is that what this is about?"

"I'm still poor!" I screamed. "Junie was poor every day of her life. It's never been about that. It's about *you*."

"If I was so terrible, if growing up here was so bad, you knew where the door was." She jutted her chin toward the front of the trailer. "Never saw you use it, though. Always seemed happy enough to keep on eating my food, sleeping under my roof."

I rolled my eyes, wishing Cal were here to catch my glance. "Oh, here we go." I braced myself for the big windup, the unappreciated, picked-on mother whose kids were ungrateful brats. It was a version of the story my mama never got tired of telling. A self-serving fairy tale studded with lies.

"What do you want me to say then?" she asked. "You want me

to apologize for seeing my own grandchild? My own flesh and blood?"

"No," I said. "Your apologies don't mean shit. We both know that. You've never been sorry for anything in your entire life. Except maybe giving birth to Cal and me."

"You're wrong," she said, her mouth twisting into a cruel little bow. "I never was sorry about Cal."

It was nothing she hadn't said to me before, but it still had the power to hurt. Not a full body blow the way it had been when I was a kid, but a quick, sharp kick to the heart. "Don't worry, Mama," I said. "You're not telling me anything I don't already know."

She turned away from me, tossed her empty beer bottle into the trash. "I ain't in the mood for this." She sighed. "I wanted to meet Junie, that's all. I meant for it to be a onetime thing. But then I got to know her." She paused, shoulder falling in a helpless shrug, the gesture you make before you admit something shameful. "I loved her," she said finally.

Nothing she could have said would have shocked me more. It was like hearing your dog start a conversation or watching the sun fall out of the sky. Something so impossible that even seeing it with your own eyes didn't make it real. "You loved her," I said, voice flat.

"I did," my mama confirmed. She sounded as surprised as anyone by the fact.

I'd known my girl was special, always had. But to unclench the tight fist of my mother? Not even Cal had ever done that. *Special* didn't even cover it. My God, I'd had no idea. I shifted in my chair, wanting to be gone, but wanting the whole story, too. This was probably my only chance. My mama wasn't one for dragging things out, peeling back the layers. Once she shut the door on this subject, it would be shut for good. "You what? Walked up to her on the street and introduced yourself? 'Hey, Junie, I'm the grandma your mom warned you about. Let's be friends'?"

"You know, I used to think I missed your real personality. The one you put on ice when Junie was born. At least that Evie had some spunk." My mama shook her head. "But it turns out I don't. Your smart-ass routine gets old quick."

I laughed, a hoarse bark. "I learned from the best. Now stop avoiding the question."

My mama leaned back against the counter, crossed her arms. "How do you think I met her? Use your brain. It ain't hard to figure out."

It took me longer than it should have, cycling through the possibilities and skipping over the most obvious one because I didn't want to believe it. "Cal?" I said finally. Voiced like a question but one I already knew the answer to. It was like taking a punch to the gut, the knowledge that Cal had violated the one trust I'd relied on him to always keep. He'd promised me. And promised Junie. Cradled her newborn body in his arms and vowed she'd always be safe, which meant keeping her far away from Mama. And he'd betrayed us both.

"Yep. I told him I deserved to meet her at least. My only grandchild." She smirked at me. "And he agreed. Didn't even put up an argument."

Of course he didn't. Because as much as Cal loved me, as much as he hated Mama, he was loyal to her, too. He still showed up at her trailer once a month with food or an envelope of cash. He visited her on Christmas Day and Mother's Day and Easter. Not like me, who before Junie died hadn't seen Mama, except from a distance, in more than five years. She had some sick hold over Cal, even now. The ability to bend him to her will when he ought to have known better. Part of me could hardly blame him for it. For all my big talk, I hadn't managed to sever that final connection, either. "If you had anything to do with what happened to Junie, if it comes back to you in even the tiniest way, Mama . . ." I let my words trail off.

"You think if I knew anything about what happened I'd be sitting here drinking beer and shooting the shit with you?" She lit up a new cigarette with a neon-pink lighter. "I don't waste time making threats, Eve." Accusatory squint through a scrim of smoke. "I don't talk. I *act*. Whoever hurt her would already be dead in a ditch."

I pushed my chair back hard, and it went over halfway, crashing into the wall behind me. "We're done," I told her. "Not for now or for today. For always. Pretend you don't know me." Even as I spoke, I had the sinking feeling my words were coming too late. Junie's death had set events in motion that couldn't be stopped. I crossed to the front door, paused before stepping out. "Pretend you never had a daughter. It shouldn't be too much of a stretch."

I wanted it to hurt her, but I knew with unflinching certainty that it hadn't. As soon as I was gone, she'd open another beer, screw the guy on the sofa, and throw a frozen dinner in the microwave. End her evening with heroin between the toes. And the daughter she'd just lost, the daughter she hadn't wanted to begin with, would never even cross her mind.

TWENTY-ONE

I couldn't face Cal yet, look him in the eye and hear his stumbling, shamefaced apology. The combination of words that would never be big enough to cover the depth of his betrayal. The worst part was, I already knew I'd forgive him. He was all I had left. My only tether to the world. And as much as I didn't want to, I understood why he'd done it. Understood how sometimes he was powerless to resist our mother. The piece of him that remained a little boy, desperate to prove his worth. But still . . . Junie. I couldn't quite wrap my head around him bringing Junie into the mix. He must have thought he could control Mama, control the way she inserted herself into Junie's life. But I knew better. There was no controlling Mama; there was only containment, and even that was fraught with danger as she constantly evaded your well-established perimeters.

She was like a weed: You'd stomp her out in one spot, but when you turned around, she'd already be growing again.

I still hadn't recovered my taste for alcohol. In truth, I probably had never had one, even when I was younger. But back then, a few too many beers had made the rest of my life easier to swallow, too. But when I passed by Jimmy Ray's strip joint, the sun beginning to fall into the horizon, I pulled into the lot. I told myself I wasn't going inside to see Jimmy Ray, that I didn't care one way or the other whether he was there, but the self-destructive song in my blood sang a different tune.

This early in the evening, the place was virtually empty. Only one stripper out on the stage and a single occupied table, two guys who eyed me as I made my way to the bar. I was surprised to see Sam working behind the counter, and it took me a second to remember that Matt was dead. Blown to smithereens right in front of my eyes.

"Hey, Eve," Sam said, shy smile easing out from under his beard. "What can I get you?"

"How about a vodka on the rocks."

Sam nodded, but kept his eyes on me a second too long. "How're you doing?" he asked as he spun a glass upright on the bar, scooped ice inside.

"Been better," I said. I didn't want to talk. I wanted to drink. And forget everything for a little while. I needed relief, and I'd take it from the bottom of a bottle if that's where I could find it.

"Jimmy Ray's not here," Sam said as he slid my drink across the bar. "He's kept himself scarce lately. Rumor has it, you about busted his nose clean off his face."

I drained half the vodka in one go, choking a little as I set the glass back down. My eyes burned, and heat spread inside my chest like tentacles. "Yep, that was me."

Sam laughed. "I would've loved to witness it." He leaned closer, lowered his voice. "But you didn't hear that from me."

I gave him what passed for a smile, finished my drink, and motioned for another. I could tell Sam wanted to say something about my newfound taste for alcohol. But this wasn't the kind of place, and we weren't the kind of people, for a *go slow, take it easy* speech. You walked in these doors to get wrecked, not to have an umbrella-adorned cocktail with your friends. I went a little slower with the second drink, but not by much. Turned around in my chair to stop Sam from trying to keep a conversation going. Of course, then I was forced to stare at the lone stripper, a woman about my own age with a greasy tangle of bottle-red hair and wide, stretch-marked hips. The tassels on her pasties swung in half-hearted arcs as she gyrated.

It wasn't until the song ended and she was climbing down off the stage that I recognized her. She'd been a brunette when I'd known her, living with her older sister a mile or two down the road. We hadn't been friends, exactly, but we'd stuck together in junior high. Not because we particularly liked each other, but because we were painfully aware that we came from the same place and there was safety in numbers. As far as I remembered, she hadn't continued on into high school.

"Hey, Crystal," I said when she got within spitting distance. There was a faint slur to my words, my voice a little higher than normal. The vodka was sitting in my gut like a sparking fire. She looked at me blankly, and I wondered if I'd gotten her name wrong. Maybe it wasn't Crystal after all, although that was a favorite in my mama's part of the world. It could have been Diamond. That one got a lot of play, too. As if the shimmer and shine of the names themselves could make up for the sad stripper lives they were destined to precede. I guess I should've counted myself lucky that my mama had picked up some Bible learning along the way and had written *Eve* on my birth certificate instead of *Sapphire* or *Destiny*.

"Oh, hey," she said finally. "Eve, right? I haven't seen you in forever."

"Yeah, it's been a while."

Crystal leaned over the bar, and I swiveled in my chair. "Can I get a Bud Light?" she asked Sam, and he nodded, handed her an icy bottle. "God." She sighed. "That tastes good. You wouldn't think it, but those lights are hot as fuck." She eyed me over her bottle. "You come in here to hang out?"

I shrugged, pointed at my glass until Sam got the hint. "Yeah."

"Huh. I can think of about half a dozen better spots. Including your own living room." She took another swig of beer. "Why in the hell would you want to spend time in this dump if you didn't have to?"

"It seemed like a good idea at the time."

That got a half smile out of her, a peek of a canine tooth and a flash of silver filling. "I hear ya. When you need a drink, you need a drink."

I didn't correct her notion that drinking was a regular habit of mine. To be fair, judging from the way I was slamming down my vodkas, she had a basis for thinking I still liked the booze. And even though I didn't enjoy the taste anymore, I was definitely enjoying the fuzziness at the edge of my vision, the blurry wall every swallow built between me and the world.

Crystal gave a quick hoot of laughter. "Remember in eighth grade when we stole a bottle from my sister, Wild Turkey or some shit, and you ended up puking in English class? I can still see the look on Mrs. Johnson's face when the smell hit her. How long did they suspend you for that time?"

"Two days." The principal had already given up on me by that point, hadn't even bothered to give me the same old lecture about getting my shit together and thinking of my future. He'd known as well as I had that I didn't have a future beyond my mama's. He probably thought I'd hit rock bottom already, but it turned out there was further to go. More suspensions for drinking and fighting in high school, a looming threat of expulsion, even a ride in the back of Land's cruiser with my hands cuffed behind my back for threatening a teacher. And then Junie came along and saved me.

Crystal pushed away her half-empty beer bottle, straightened one of her tassels with a practiced hand. "I thought maybe you were in here looking for your brother, but I haven't seen him lately."

"Wait, what?" I said, words stumbling and slow. "My brother doesn't come in here."

"Sure he does," Crystal said, going to work on her other tassel, untangling the shimmery black threads. She glanced over at me. "I mean, not to stuff dollar bills in my crotch or anything."

I shook my head, thinking that might clear away the alcohol cobwebs, but the room tilted and spun. "My brother?" My words were more than slightly slurred now, the syllables running together in one long exhalation. "Cal?"

"That's who we're talking about," Crystal said. "Good-looking. Cop." She made a gun of her fingers and pulled the trigger in illustration. "Whoa, easy." She grabbed my shoulder. "You definitely can't hold your liquor, can you?"

"I'm not . . ." I palmed hair off my face. "I'm not used to drinking." I jerked away from her hand, caught myself on the edge of the bar when I almost toppled off the stool. "What was Cal doing in here?"

Crystal didn't touch me again, but her hand hovered nearby, ready to catch me if I pitched forward. "Well, that's beyond my pay grade. I'm not exactly privy to what goes on in here that doesn't involve tits and ass. But he was always huddling with that Matt guy. The asshole who got himself blown all to hell a few days ago? That's as much as I know."

I would have given anything to wipe away the inability to focus that I'd been loving only a second before. Nothing that Crystal was saying made sense, and I couldn't clear my brain enough to put any pieces together.

"Gotta go," she said. "You gonna be okay?"

"Yeah, but wait," I managed. "Stay for a second."

"No can do," Crystal said, already walking away. "It's my song."

I watched as she sashayed across the floor, cheap stilettos tapping, and climbed back up to the stage. A mask dropped over her face as she stood, her eyes going blank and faraway. I caught Sam's attention by slamming my glass down on the bar, and he hurried over, his eyebrows pinching together.

"Did you hear that?" I asked him. "What she said about my brother and Matt?"

"No," Sam said. "But I wouldn't put too much stock in anything Crystal says. She's not the most reliable person. Likes to stir up shit." He wiped down the bar in front of me. "Can I get you a water?"

I stared at my empty glass. Water was what I needed, but it wasn't what I wanted. I wanted oblivion. For the first time since Junie died, the pain felt distant. Not gone, but not a raw, exposed wound, either. Hidden behind a semi-opaque wall. I could see its outlines, but not its details. So I had a fourth vodka. And maybe a fifth. I don't remember. My last coherent memory was my forehead resting on the bar, my stomach rolling, a bead of sweat down my back, a man's voice in my ear. And then nothing.

. . .

I woke up naked, between cotton sheets. A ceiling fan whirling above my head. Popcorn ceiling with a watermark in the corner. I knew that ceiling. I knew that fan. Fuck. I turned my head, and Jimmy Ray looked back at me from the opposite pillow. I stayed still, like maybe if I didn't move, didn't acknowledge him, I could go back to sleep, wake up a second time and be somewhere else.

"Hey, Eve," he said. "You look like hell."

"Thanks," I muttered. I stretched out my leg, froze when it brushed up against his.

Jimmy Ray hooted out a laugh that pierced my skull. "You should see your face right now. You'd think this was the first time you'd ever been naked in my bed."

I closed my eyes, forced my aching brain to remember. I got only bits and pieces, shimmery and vague. A hand under my legs, lifting me. The slam of a car door. My arm tangled in my bra strap and my laughter, loud and crazed. Jimmy Ray's face moving closer, my hand curled around the back of his neck.

"I was drunk," I said. My voice was thick and hoarse, my stomach caught somewhere in my throat.

"Yep," Jimmy Ray said. "Wasted." He nudged me with his knee. "Never seen you like that before."

"And you never will again." I pushed myself upright, one hand holding the sheet to my chest. I rested my forehead on my bent knees. Baby steps.

"You were definitely looking to get wrecked." Jimmy Ray ran a finger down my back, bumping over my spine. I hated myself for not hating his touch. "Was it about Junie?" He asked the question so quietly, so sincerely, that I looked over my shoulder to see if he was screwing with me. But his face was solemn, his eyes steady on mine.

"Everything's about Junie," I told him. Saying her name sparked something, like a lit match that sputters in your fingers, not quite sure if it's going to take. I pressed my fingers against my temples, not sure if I was willing the memory of last night to gel into some-thing solid or hoping it would disappear into the shadowy corridors of my mind. "I saw my mama yesterday. She spent time with Junie. Did you know that?"

"Yeah. I saw 'em in the Bait & Tackle a time or two. They were two peas in a pod, always huddled together in the back corner."

"Doing what?" I'd swung toward him too fast and had to put one hand down on the bed to steady myself, bile rising. "What were they talking about?"

"Hell, girl, I don't know. Eavesdropping on them wasn't top pri-ority for me." He paused, thinking. "I did hear Lynette telling Junie that she'd never finished junior high, that she wasn't much for book learning. She was encouraging Junie to keep up with her studies, far as I could tell." He shrugged. "Seemed harmless to me."

I raised my eyebrows. "My mama is never harmless. You know that. I can't believe you didn't tell me about seeing them together."

"We haven't exactly been on speaking terms these past few years," he reminded me. "Hell, if I even tried to say hello, you hit me with the stink eye before I could get a word out. And as I recall, Land gave me a pretty stern talking-to after our last fight. Told me to mind my own business where you were concerned. Besides, far as I knew, it wasn't a secret that Junie and your mama saw each other. They were kin, weren't they?" Jimmy Ray reached behind him with one hand, pulled his pillow up a little and settled back down. "That's what brought you into my place last night? You wanted to ride my ass about your mama and Junie knowing each other?" He sounded dubious, at best.

"I wasn't looking for you, if that's what you're thinking," I said, wanting to wipe the smirk right off his face. It didn't work. Maybe because I'd still ended up in his bed, one way or the other. "I'm not sure why I was there. I wanted to forget everything for a little while, I guess." I paused, pulling on my memories again, worrying at the threads. Knowing this road was nowhere I really wanted to go, but helpless to stop walking it. Because in the light of day, Junie loomed large again. The pain was back, full throttle, and with it the anger. Burning and boiling below the surface. "I talked to Crystal while I was there."

"Crystal." Jimmy Ray snorted. "Pretty accurate name given her meth habit."

"She said something about Matt and Cal." I hoped he would contradict Crystal, tell me she was full of shit. "That they were always talking. Hanging out. Or something."

"You'll have to ask your brother about that," Jimmy Ray said after a pause that went on a little too long.

My heart plummeted, left a hollow, aching void in my chest. "You're saying it's true?"

Jimmy Ray shook his head. "I'm not saying shit. I'm saying you'll have to talk to your brother if you want answers to a question like that."

"Fine," I said, "that's what I'll do." I slid my legs to the edge of the bed. I took a deep breath, grabbed my underwear and jeans from the floor, and pulled them on, ignoring Jimmy Ray's eyes on my bare ass. *Nothing he hasn't seen before*, I told myself. *Last night, in fact, if we're keeping track.* "By the way, weren't you the one telling me I wasn't asking the right questions a few days ago? 'Follow the money, Eve,' isn't that what you told me? And now, suddenly, you've got nothing to say?"

"Nope," Jimmy Ray said. He sounded amused.

"Where's my bra?" I asked, turning to face him with one arm over my breasts.

"Around here somewhere." He grinned at me. "You're crazy if you think I'm helping you find it. I'm enjoying the show too much."

"You're disgusting," I told him. Threw aside blankets and kicked through piles on the floor until I found it, then my shirt wadded into a ball next to his dresser. "Can you give me a ride back to my car?"

"No need. It's right out front. I had Sam drive it over last night."

Vintage Jimmy Ray. On the surface it seemed like a thoughtful gesture, but really it was insurance against me outstaying my welcome. I leaned over to pick up my shoes, still moving slowly to keep my stomach from sliding into my mouth, and Jimmy Ray reached out, locked his hand around my wrist. I jerked upright, shoes forgotten, tried to pull away.

"Sit," he said, giving my arm a tug. I pulled backward, but he tightened his grip. "Sit," he repeated, less give in his voice this time, patting the bed next to his hip with his free hand. "For a second."

I sat gingerly, the edge of my butt touching the bed, my whole body wound tight and poised for flight. I didn't think he was in a hitting mood, but with Jimmy Ray you could never tell for sure. He sighed, like I was being ridiculous, but he let go of my wrist, made himself comfortable again on his stack of pillows. "Remember Libby Lang?" he asked me.

"Yeah," I said. "Of course I do." When I was growing up, people told the story of Libby Lang with a kind of predatory glee, the same way I suspected city kids told stories of girls snatched off the street by strangers or houses haunted by killer ghosts. A mythical legend meant to warn, but also to titillate. It didn't matter if the story was true; what mattered was the lesson. *Don't be like Libby. Don't let it happen to you.* All of it always blowing back on Libby, everyone else involved somehow wiped crystal clean of any blame. The story was always a little different depending on who told it, but in the version I heard most often Libby was raised by her mama in a trailer not far from where I grew up. She was one of eight or ten kids—the number changed with the teller. All of them with different daddies— that part of the story never varied. But when Libby was about twelve or thirteen, she got a wild hair up her ass to find her real daddy. Maybe she was tired of whoever her mama had playing the role at the time, some loser with meaty fists or wandering hands. Or maybe she was one of those fanciful girls, the kind who entertain stories about how somewhere out there is a real family who will save them, cuddle them, and treat them like the princesses they were meant to be. A fool, in other words. The only link Libby had to her father was her paternal grandma, a woman she saw maybe once or twice a year. When Libby asked about her father, her grandma warned her off. Told her that he didn't have no interest in knowing Libby, that he wasn't a good man. Which, given the rumors about Libby's granny, seems like advice Libby might've wanted to heed. If that woman—who bred fighting dogs and threw her own children out like leftover trash—thought someone was bad news, then he surely was. But Libby was stubborn, and she kept asking around. Sticking her nose in where it didn't belong. This is the point in the story when everyone's voice dropped, the words coming out more like a hiss. Eventually, she found out where her daddy was holed up deep in the holler (making moonshine or meth—again it depended on who told the story) and Libby took off to find him. Everyone knew it wouldn't come to anything good, and they were proved right when she showed back up a month or so later, beaten half to death, missing a finger, and pregnant. The thing was, no one around here had any sympathy for Libby, who should have known better. There are consequences to digging too much, to trying to find people who don't want to be found, to not taking no for an answer. To pushing past your limits. Libby was the poster child for I told you so. The wretched face next to the definition of she had it coming.

"That story's probably not even true," I said. "Just some made up bullshit to keep us all in line."

"It's true," Jimmy Ray said. "I knew her. She was my age." His voice was serious along with his face, lines etched around his mouth. "She had the baby and then she killed it. Killed herself, too. Drank a bottle of bleach. She thought she knew what she could handle, how much she could take. But she was wrong."

Goose bumps prickled the back of my neck, and I crossed my arms, cupped my elbows against a sudden chill. "Don't worry," I said. "I'm nothing like Libby Lang. She was a kid. I'm a grown woman."

"Pain don't discriminate, Eve. It doesn't know if you're grown. Doesn't care, either. It hits as hard either way. Libby wanted to know who her daddy was, but she would have been better off leaving well enough alone." Jimmy Ray leaned forward, green eyes glittering in the dark purple shadows around his still healing nose. "Sometimes the answers are worse than the questions. Sometimes it's better not to know."

"I have to," I whispered. I didn't know how to explain it to him, this man who'd never loved anyone, not really. How Junie might not be in the world anymore, but that didn't make her any less present. She was entwined with every part of me. Every muscle, every drop of blood in my body, every breath I took, every thought and wish and memory. I couldn't put all that away, keep going and forget about what had been done to her. Couldn't be such a coward that I shied away from the truth, even if it was the killing kind.

"Okay, suit yourself," Jimmy Ray said, wiping his hands of it, of me. He threw himself back on the pillows, watched as I stood and slipped on my shoes. "Am I gonna see you around here again?"

"No," I said. Whichever way this went, from here on out, Jimmy Ray and I were over. I had a feeling I'd find my self-destruction somewhere else soon enough.

TWENTY-TWO

I made it as far as my car, slid in behind the wheel, before I ran out of energy. My head throbbed in time with my heartbeat, and my tongue lay thick and foreign in my mouth. I closed my eyes, forcing back the sting of tears, as the first rays of daylight peeked over the horizon. I couldn't remember ever being this tired, this down-to-the-bone exhausted, not even in those early weeks after Junie was born. Maybe Jimmy Ray was right. Maybe it was time to let things lie, stop poking around like a dumb kid messing with a nest of rattlers. Junie might even forgive me for giving up. But I knew I wouldn't forgive myself, that I'd never have a true peaceful moment until I saw this through to the end. I opened my eyes and started the car.

My first instinct was to confront Cal, step right into his face and ask him what in the hell was going on. But I remembered his expression that day by the river when I'd basically accused him of messing around with Izzy. If I made another misstep like that, leaped without evidence, I wasn't sure we'd recover. And underneath that worry was a new one, a consideration I'd never really had before with Cal: He might look directly into my eyes and lie to me. I needed to figure this out before I confronted him, nail the facts down tight without any wiggle room.

Problem was, I wasn't sure where to start. The answer came to me lumbering through the parking lot of the diner when I drove past. Land, hitching up his pants and heading inside for a predawn cup of joe. And, judging from his ever-growing belly, probably a piece of cherry pie to go with it.

I swung into the lot, pulled to a stop right in front of him, and leaned across the passenger seat to roll down the window.

"Jesus, Eve," Land said, bending down to look at me, one arm braced on the roof of my car. "About took off the tips of my toes."

"Sorry," I said, and he rolled his eyes at my dismissive tone. "I was wondering if you've heard anything new about the case?"

"Nothing we're ready to share just yet."

"What does that mean?"

Land sighed. "We're working it as hard as we can, Eve." I heard the frustration in his tone and the sincerity, too. It shocked me a little. Sometimes I forgot that Land might actually care about who killed Junie and Izzy beyond wanting to clear it off his books. "Wish I had more to tell you, I really do."

"What about Matt?" I asked, throwing out my bait to see what I might catch.

Land jerked back a little, scowl on his face. "Matt? You mean the one dumb enough to mess around with Izzy Logan and then get himself blown to bits?"

A tiny pulse started ticking in my stomach. "Yeah," I said, careful.

"He didn't have nothing to do with the murders," Land said, leaning closer now. "I sure do wish I'd had a chance to talk to him about his sniffing around Izzy. I woulda made sure he never pulled something like that again. But he was working a shift at the strip joint when the girls died. Half a dozen witnesses, at least. He had an alibi as tight as those pants he wore."

The pulse in my stomach ballooned and bottomed out, leaving a hollow pit behind. What had Cal said when I'd asked him about talking to Matt? *He tried denying it at first, but we kept pressing him.* Cal and Land talking to Matt about his relationship with Izzy. But here Land was, knowing nothing about it. It was such a small, stupid lie. And yet I couldn't think of any reason Cal would tell it unless it was hiding something bigger and uglier.

"You been thinking Matt was the one who killed the girls?" Land asked. "I can see where you might jump to that conclusion after the business with him and Izzy. But like I said, it wasn't him."

"I guess I thought maybe he was involved. Knew something. That's why I was asking." I was rambling, words butting up against each other, and I forced myself to take a breath and relax. "Seems like a lot of people dying around here recently. I made a leap I probably shouldn't have, that's all." I tried on a smile. "That's what happens when you can't sleep. You lie there overthinking everything."

Land stared at me for a moment. "Huh," he said finally. "Well, try and get some rest, Eve. We'll let you know when we've got something, all right?"

"Okay." I nodded. "Thanks."

Land knocked twice on my roof in response and then edged around the front of my car and into the diner. It was the first time in years I didn't have the urge to hurt him.

. . .

I waited until Cal left for work, watched him pull away from the curb and head west toward the police station. I'd parked a block away from his low-slung duplex, but still huddled down until I barely cleared the dashboard, although from what I could tell Cal never once glanced my way.

I'd let myself into Cal's place a hundred times over the years. I had his key right next to my own on my worn key ring. But this morning felt different, covert and suspect. I didn't exactly slink up to his doorway, but it wasn't my usual casual stroll, either. I was very aware of myself and the world around me, the sound of my footsteps, the wind through the trees, the open blinds in Cal's living room window, the sun hitting the back of my neck. The other half of Cal's duplex was occupied by an elderly woman who rarely came outside. The most contact Cal generally had with her was when she banged on their shared wall when he had a football game turned up too loud. I didn't think she'd be paying much attention to my approach. Still, I let myself in quickly, didn't really take an easy breath until I had the door closed and locked behind me.

"This is stupid," I said under my breath. What did I think I was doing? What did I actually think I was going to find? Crystal probably wasn't even right about Cal hanging out with Matt. And there was probably a totally logical explanation for why Cal had lied about him and Land talking to Matt about Izzy. None of it had to *mean* anything. *But what if it does?* my mind whispered.

Cal's place was nicer than mine by objective standards, bigger, slightly more updated. But he used it only as a place to shower and sleep, a way station. He spent most of his time at work or, before Junie died, at my apartment. There wasn't much that marked this place as Cal's. No desk with overflowing drawers or shelves of knickknacks perfect for concealment. I started in the kitchen, although it seemed an unlikely spot for anything suspect. It didn't help that I had no idea what I was looking for. But half the kitchen drawers were empty, and the other half held standard kitchen fare: a spatula, a whisk with the tag still attached, a pot holder Junie had crocheted as a Christmas present a few years ago.

I moved on to Cal's bedroom, ran my hand over the pale oak headboard and matching dresser I'd helped him pick out when he'd first moved in. He hadn't cared about what we got, seemed content to sleep with his mattress on the floor and his clothes stored in milk crates, but I wanted him to have something homey, something to help turn this bland beige box of a room into his personal space. But other than the furniture, he'd never done much. No art on the walls. No clutter on the nightstand. Only a single framed picture of Junie and me on top of his dresser, both of us laughing, my arms encircling her from behind. Looking at Cal's room made me sad in a way I couldn't quite put my finger on. It was too empty, too blank. Like a life that was never fully lived.

I'd always used the space between my mattress and box springs as my hiding place when I was a kid. Not the most ingenious hiding place, but I never had much to hide to begin with. But Cal had always been cleverer. Like me, he hadn't had much worth squirreling away, but when he did, he went to great lengths to make sure it wouldn't be found. I checked all the obvious spots, but I didn't hold out much hope of finding anything there.

Eventually I ended up in his closet, reaching my hands into the corners of his high shelf and then on the floor, running my fingers along the baseboards. I'd about given up when I felt the edge of the carpet pulled away from the floor. I tugged and it came up easily, exposing a square of subfloor that had been cut out at some point and then replaced. I sat back on my heels, heart galloping, sweat slicking my palms. Did I want to lift up that piece of flooring? How badly did I want answers?

"Stop being a chickenshit," I said, my voice too loud in the stillness. I tried using my bare hands to get the square of plywood up, but had to dig out my keys and use one to pry up an edge enough to slip my finger into the gap. The square came out easily after that, and I peered carefully into the dark space below. I didn't see anything and I hoped maybe I was wrong. Maybe this was a remnant from the builder. Maybe this hidey-hole had nothing to do with my brother at all.

I reached a hand down, wincing a little in anticipation of bugs or rats, but my fingers butted up against something smooth and cool. I pulled it out. A freezer-sized ziplock bag filled with cash. A sound came out of me, a moaning kind of cry, and I dropped onto my stomach, reached my whole arm into the space. By the time I was done, there were seven bags of cash on the floor next to me. Thousands of dollars. More money than I'd ever seen in my life.

Follow the money. Well, here it was, spread out next to me on Cal's closet floor, but I couldn't quite put it together with Junie's death. Partly because I didn't see how it fit and partly because I couldn't stand to click the final pieces together. I was making a low, animal humming sound in the back of my throat, and I forced myself to take deep, even breaths until I stopped. I clicked through possibilities in my mind, trying to find one that slotted into place. Cal and Matt stealing money from Jimmy Ray, maybe? Junie killed as a kind of punishment? But then why would Jimmy Ray point me toward the money, and his own guilt? Maybe Cal was stealing directly from

Matt and he went after Junie. Sent someone to deliver the message while he worked at the strip joint hiding behind his alibi.

I sat up, leaned back against Cal's closet wall. I needed to talk to him, figure out what role he'd played in all this. Because there was no denying now that he was involved, somehow. I leaned forward, reaching to replace the piece of subfloor, and caught a glint of light from the dark hole. Something I'd missed, something shimmering. My brain knew what it was immediately, but my heart refused to believe it until I had it out of the hole, held right up next to my face. A phone. With a pink glitter case and a cracked screen. Izzy's missing phone. I'd seen her texting on it dozens of times. Izzy's lost phone hidden away in Cal's house. There was no explanation for it, no reason he could possibly give for having it that didn't end with two girls dead in the snow.

I thought about the text Izzy had gotten on her phone that morning, luring her to her death. Jimmy Ray's black eye from Cal, and my too-quick assumption that he was interrogating Jimmy Ray when maybe he'd really been covering his own ass. The way Cal steered me away from Jimmy Ray's advice to follow the money, subtle and delicate, but maneuvering me just the same. How fast he'd shown up after Matt's trailer had blown up, there practically as soon as the explosion lit up the sky. Because he'd been there all along, I realized. Had killed Matt to keep me from finding out what he knew, to keep Land from asking Matt all the right questions.

The walls of the closet moved closer to me and then away, rippling like waves, and I lowered my head down between my knees. Up until this moment, some part of me had still hoped that maybe it was only the money. That whatever Cal had been involved with, however bad it was, didn't relate directly to the girls' deaths. But the phone changed everything. The phone was proof that the person I trusted most in the world was responsible for my daughter's death. Now I had to figure out what I was brave enough to do about it.

. . .

Zach smiled when he opened his front door and saw it was me, but it didn't quite reach his eyes. "Hey," he said, "Come on in." He stood back to usher me inside. He didn't move farther into the house, though, and his gaze darted toward the kitchen and then away. For my part, I was so jittery that I bounced up and down on my toes, my eyes swinging from him to the door, back and forth, back and forth. All I could think about was the time I was wasting. But for some reason I couldn't even name, I felt like I owed him this chance.

"So," he said when I'd turned down his half-hearted offer of coffee. "What's up?"

"I know who did it," I said. I'd meant to ease into it, not vomit it at his feet, but everything inside me was fizzing and popping, out of control.

Zach stared at me, the color draining from his face. "What?"

I flapped a hand through the air, watched it like it wasn't actually a part of my body. "I mean, it's possible he didn't actually do it. But he was involved in it."

"Who?" The question came out on a limp puff of air.

"Cal," I said, forcing the word from my throat.

Zach's whole face scrunched up, blank with incomprehension. "Your brother? But he's a cop."

"I'm aware," I said, impatient with this part of it. I wanted to fast-forward through all the *how? what? why?* questions. The truth was, I didn't have answers to any of them. And Jimmy Ray had been right. When it came down to it, I didn't care about the why. I only cared about the who. "I'm going to talk to him. Do you want to come with me?"

"Me . . . what . . . what about the cops? The other cops. Shouldn't we be calling Land right now?" He turned toward the kitchen, and I grabbed at his arm.

"No. We're not telling anyone. Not yet."

"What are you *talking* about?" Zach's voice was rising with each word, and I pushed down with my hand, trying to silence him.

"Calm down," I said. "We'll tell them soon. But I want to talk to him first. He's my brother. I want to hear what he has to say before Land and a bunch of lawyers get in the middle of it."

Zach forced out a laugh, ran a hand through his hair, leaving it standing up in uneven tufts. "What, you're going to go all vigilante on his ass? Is that your big plan?"

"I didn't say anything about going after him. I just want to talk," I said again. "I think I'm allowed that much."

"I don't . . ." He sank down onto the bench near the front door. I stayed quiet, let him work through it for a second. "It seems like a really bad idea, Eve," he said finally.

"Maybe," I admitted. A noise in the hall caught my attention, the whisper-light sound of a footstep. But when I turned, no one was there.

"What if he hurts you?"

I turned back to Zach. "I don't think he will." Of course, before today I would have bet anything, risked anything, on the idea that Cal would never hurt Junie. That he'd take a bullet before he'd harm a hair on her head. So it was entirely possible that I was wrong. The thing was, I didn't much care. "Look, I didn't come here for your permission or your blessing. But you were her father. I thought you had a right to know, and I wanted to give you the chance to come with me."

Zach stared into his coffee mug like the right answer might be hidden in its depths. "I don't think so," he said. "This isn't me, Eve. It's not how I handle things. I won't say anything to Land. Or Jenny. At least not yet. But I won't go with you, either."

In truth, it was exactly the answer I'd been expecting. The one I wanted, really. Because it proved, after everything, that I had been right. Junie had never been his. She'd always been solely and completely mine.

. . .

"Well, damn," my mama said when she pushed open her trailer door, still dressed in the same clothes as the last time I'd seen her. "Wasn't it just yesterday that you told me to forget I had a daughter? So who the hell are you? I don't allow strangers on my property." She smirked at her own cleverness.

This moment was the one that would decide everything. If I crossed her doorstep, asked for her help, trusted her, there was no going back. No pretending ever again that I was anything other than my mother's daughter. No better than her. No different.

"Let me in, Mama," I told her. "We need to talk."

TWENTY-THREE

I was sitting on a rock next to the river when he found me. I'd been watching the water flow past for over an hour, lost in the ripples and eddies, the occasional silver flash of a fish's scales. I was surprised when I looked up and saw that the sun was slipping through the late-afternoon sky, its edge kissing the horizon and lighting it up with streamers of pink.

"Hey," Cal said. "What's going on? You've got Mama worked up into a tizzy. And you know that takes some doing."

I could barely look at him; hearing his voice was bad enough. Reminding me of all our childhood hours. The times he'd fed me when I was hungry, comforted me when I was hurt, reassured me when I was terrified. Cal, who I loved more than myself. More than anyone but Junie.

He sat next to me, and I could feel his eyes on my face, smell his shampoo when the breeze kicked up. "Are you okay?" he asked. "I kind of freaked out when Mama showed up and said I needed to get out here. I think she thought you might have . . ." He gestured toward the river, where water crashed over rock in an endless spill.

I didn't say anything. Pulled Izzy's phone from my jacket pocket and set it on the ground between us.

Cal inhaled once, sharp and fast, scrambled backward on his butt like I'd put down a grenade instead of a cell phone. "Listen," he said, voice high and trembling "I can explain it. I can—"

I turned and looked at him. "You can explain how Izzy Logan's phone ended up hidden in your house, or you can explain why you killed them?"

Cal's mouth opened, then closed, then opened again, but nothing came out. He looked like one of the countless fish he'd caught and gutted right at this very spot, and I felt the insane urge to laugh. And I knew from the look in his eyes that my worst fear was true. He'd been the one to wield the knife after all.

"I didn't mean to," he said finally. "It happened fast. It all got away from me. So fast." His voice broke, and fat tears spilled down his cheeks. He covered his face with both hands and wept. I turned back to the river, watched the wind ruffle through the grass on the far side. I could be patient. I could let him cry, and talk, and explain. None of it mattered because this was already ending only one way.

"Please," he said, reached out and laid a hand on my arm. I looked down at his fingers, imagined breaking each one until he let go. "Let me . . . let me tell you what happened. It's not what you think."

I nodded, even though I was pretty sure it was exactly what I thought. He'd valued something more than Junie's life. End of story. But the sooner he started talking, the sooner he'd be done.

"I was doing it for her. For Junie."

That surprised me, and my head whipped in his direction. "Doing *what* for Junie?"

"The money. I wanted her to be able to leave this place, go to college, something. Get out. But what I make isn't enough, not even close. And one night I ran into Matt and he started saying how Land had been giving them some hassle about how big the operation was getting. How they could really use someone on the inside to help things run a little more smoothly. At first I told myself I was only listening. I wasn't actually going to do anything. But then I talked to Jimmy Ray and it seemed like a perfect deal." He shrugged. "They were selling the drugs anyway. Whether I helped or not. Why not gain something from it? It's not like I was stealing from babies. It seemed like a fair trade."

What did people around here always say? That you could take the kid out of the holler, but you could never take the holler out of the kid. I hadn't wanted to believe it, but Cal and I were living proof. Dress us up in a cop uniform, give us a child to care for, and we might walk the straight and narrow for a while. But our history always rose up to meet us. Or dragged us down to its level. That night in the bar, Cal had been right. We were exactly who Mama'd raised us to be.

"And it was going fine," Cal continued. "I was making good money. Socking it away for Junie. I never spent any of it."

"Were you ever going to tell me?" I asked.

"Yeah, sure. But not until it was time for her to use it. I figured you wouldn't object as much if the money was right there when she needed it. And by then I planned to be done with all that, anyway."

If he actually believed that, then he had no real idea about how Jimmy Ray worked. He never would have let Cal walk away. "She didn't need money from you," I told him. "She could have gotten a scholarship if she wanted to go to college, or I could have figured something out." But we both knew I couldn't have. As much as I'd loved my daughter, there were some things I never would have been able to give her, no matter how much I wanted to. As Mama liked to say, you couldn't get blood from a stone.

"I didn't want her to leave here poor. Go to college and have everyone know she came from nothing. I wanted her to have a leg up, the way we never did. That way she'd have had a fighting chance at something better. And it was going fine, just like I planned. But then Izzy took a liking to Matt. I was the one who introduced them. Can you believe that shit? I was talking to Matt in front of the laundromat, and Izzy wandered by, stopped to say hi to me." He shook his head. "You have no idea how many times I've gone over it. Over it and over it on nights I can't sleep. How that one thing, that one *stupid* thing, ruined it all."

"I think you're the one who ruined it all." My voice was cold and hard and didn't sound like me at all. Or at least not the me my daughter would have recognized.

"I didn't mean to," Cal said again, and my hand tingled with the urge to punch him. "It was all such a huge clusterfuck. I was over at Matt's, sorting drugs and counting money, and Izzy barged right into his trailer. She's lucky she even made it that far, hitched a ride out on the highway." He shook his head. "I thought maybe it was still okay. She was young, maybe she didn't even know what she was seeing. But her mouth dropped open and her eyes went wide and all I could think about was her telling Junie and Junie telling you and everything falling apart. I'd lose my job. Land would be so pissed I'd gone behind his back that he'd push for criminal charges. It would all be ruined. I talked to Izzy. Told her how important it was to keep quiet. And how I wouldn't say anything to anyone about her and Matt, either. We'd do each other a favor."

"And she went along with it?"

Cal nodded. "Yeah. But I could tell it wasn't going to hold. I talked to her a few times around town, and she hinted about wanting to tell Junie. I knew she wasn't going to be able to keep it a secret forever. She didn't have it in her. I think she liked the idea of having something she could use to hurt Junie with. You know how teenage girls can be, petty and jealous. She'd talked a few times about how she thought her dad liked Junie more than her. Someday when she was feeling slighted it was going to come bursting out of her, a way to take Junie down a peg."

"Because Junie idolized you," I said, voice flat. "Thought you were her perfect Uncle Cal."

Cal breathed in a watery sob. "All Izzy had to do was keep her mouth shut. That's all she had to do."

"And she wasn't going to, so you decided to kill her."

"*No*," Cal said, fierce. "No. I only wanted to talk to her. I texted her on a burner phone. Asked her to meet me at the park."

"When it was snowing. And no one else was around."

"Yeah, but only because I didn't want anyone to see us together, not for a conversation this serious. I had no idea Junie was even there. We met behind that tunnel, and I didn't even see Junie. Izzy must have told her to wait somewhere else in the park." He drew in a shuddering breath. "I thought I could convince her, but she said Junie deserved to know. I don't even think she cared that much. She liked having a secret, knowing something no one else did and holding it over my head."

"She was twelve, Cal. She wasn't some criminal mastermind out to ruin your life."

"I know that," he said. "I know that now. But in the moment I was pissed and panicking and she wouldn't listen to me. She never listened! I swear to God, I didn't even know what I'd done until I saw the blood." He looked down at his hand. "There was blood all over my arm, and I thought, *What the fuck?* I didn't even know where it had come from at first."

"Bullshit," I said, flat. "For someone who went there with no plans to hurt anyone, that knife sure came in handy."

"I *always* have my knife," he said. "Every second person who lives around here has the same thing in their back pocket. I didn't plan on using it. I swear, Evie, I didn't. I took it out to scare her, that's it. I thought that would be enough. But she was going to ruin me. She was going to open her mouth and fuck it all up. I'd risked everything—my job, my relationship with you and Junie, my freedom—and she didn't even care. All I could think about was stopping her."

"What about what you did to Junie?" I asked, and the world went still. The sun lowered in the sky, and a shadow skimmed across our faces.

Cal lowered his head into his hands, spoke through his fingers. "I had no idea she was there. None at all. Izzy never said a word about bringing Junie along. I was standing there, watching Izzy bleed out, wondering what the hell had happened, and I heard a noise behind me. I reacted, turned with that knife in my hand. That's all it was. Some animal instinct. I didn't even realize it was Junie until it was too late, until I'd already . . ." He breathed in deep, his lungs stuttering on a sob. "I never would have hurt her intentionally, Eve. Never. Not Junie." He raised his head and looked at me through tear-bright eyes. "I stayed with her. Until the end. I held her hand and told her it would be okay."

"Is that supposed to make me feel better?" I asked, my own tears threatening. "Because it doesn't. Not even a little bit." Almost as bad as knowing the truth was the realization of how badly I wanted to believe him. I didn't doubt for a second that on any other day, in any other circumstance, he would have laid down his life for Junie. And I could picture it playing out exactly as he'd said: the split-second reaction, that hair-trigger instinct our mama had ingrained in us whenever we smelled danger. Kill or be killed. By the time he understood what he'd done, it was already over. Whether he'd realized that it was Junie or not, he was only doing what he'd been taught. And now, so was I.

"I'll turn myself in," Cal said. "Right now. If that's what you want."

"That's not what I want," I told him.

"Okay," he said, nodding. "Okay, then how do I make it right?"

"There's no making it right. You can't rewind time, Cal. You can't bring them back." I raised my right hand, the one he hadn't seen yet, the one that was holding a gun, and laid it across my knees. "There's only making it even."

It gave me a certain dark satisfaction to watch his eyes go wide, see his cheeks pale. He started to push up from the ground, and I raised the gun, steady and sure. "Don't," I told him. He didn't, dropped back down to sitting. He knew about me and guns. How good I was. Hell, I'd learned at his knee.

"What are you doing, Evie?" he asked.

"I think you know." I thumbed the safety off and watched his gaze follow the movement. "Even if what you did to Junie was an accident, all this time, you let me wonder what happened. You let me think Junie was keeping secrets from me about Izzy. You let me drive myself crazy about the explosion at Matt's trailer, when it was you who'd lit the match. You let me feel guilty for accusing you of being Izzy's older guy when you'd actually done something so much worse. I told you, I told everyone at that press conference, what I'd do when I found the person who killed her. You had fair warning."

When Cal swallowed, his Adam's apple bobbed like he'd swallowed a rock. I wondered how hard his heart was hammering. Mine felt even and smooth as glass. "This is me, Evie," he said. "I fucked up. I know I did. But you can't kill me."

"Sure I can." The conversational tone of my voice surprised even me. I raised the gun, close enough there was no chance of missing him. A sure-thing target.

"Where'd you get the gun?" he asked, voice quiet. He already knew, but he wanted to make me say it.

"Mama," I said, after a pause. "Because you made a mistake, Cal. One of many, as it turns out. You introduced her to Junie. The one thing I asked you never to do. The one thing you *promised* me you never would. The day Junie was born, you held my hand in the hospital, you looked into my eyes, and you swore to me you'd never let Mama get near her. We were going to stop it from happening all over again. Stop her from ever getting her claws into Junie. But you lied." He opened his mouth to speak, and I shushed him by tightening my finger on the trigger. "And guess what? Mama loved my girl. She loved her more than me. More than you. More than anything. When she found out what you'd done? She couldn't give me this gun fast enough. And you know Mama, this gun's passed through so many hands, it's probably untraceable. She's already got a story all cooked up for where you are, what happened to you."

"God," Cal said, shaking his head. "You and Mama. I should have known she'd get there in the end." He looked up at me, eyes shimmering with tears. "Stay away from her, Evie, if you can. Promise me you won't let her get too close."

I gave him a sharp-edged grin. "I think we've already established that promises don't mean shit when it comes to Mama."

Cal shook off my words, his voice strained. "Promise me. She'll drag you down to hell if you let her."

"It doesn't matter anymore, Cal." I gestured between us with the gun. "I'm already there."

I watched as tears slid down his cheeks. He reached out with careful fingers and grasped my free hand. "It's always been you and me, Evie. Remember? Always."

I thought of all the nights we spent as kids, huddled together on the edge of our property, waiting out Mama's drug-fueled parties. We stayed far away, enough that the greasy spill of light from the trailer windows didn't reach us. We made promises to each other in the inky blackness, hands twined together like the branches over-head. *We'll get out of here. Both of us. I won't leave you behind. I'll always trust you. I'll always keep you safe. Always.* Cal's pale blue eyes glimmering in the moonlight. The breeze sending strands of golden-blond hair skating across his face. We were more than siblings; we were each other's lifeline. Together, we survived a childhood designed to destroy.

The things we said to each other on those endless nights, against the ugly backdrop of our probable futures, weren't just words. Each syllable reeked of power, left our mouths heavy with intent. Our promises lifted up into the night air, through wet, humid steam, on puffy clouds of breath, through all the months and seasons. The words didn't belong to us alone; they had been released into the world. We had been heard. *Both of us. Always.* The sacred weight of vows.

And yet, they'd been only words after all. Because here we were, destroying each other anyway. And it was so much easier than it should have been. My lips trembled, and my dead heart cracked open. Tempting as it was to lay all this at our mama's feet, that wouldn't be fair. She'd shown us the path, but we'd both chosen to walk it. No one dragged that knife across my daughter's throat but Cal. No one pointed this gun but me.

"I love you, Evie," Cal said, squeezed my hand and let go. He could have been ten again, tucking me into bed. Trying to reassure me that everything would be okay, even when we both knew that it wouldn't.

"I love you, too," I told him. "Always."

The dying sun lit him up like a corona, glinting off his hair. He smiled at me, small and sad. And then I blew him away.

TWENTY-FOUR

I sat next to him until it was dark, held his hand until his fingers began to grow cold, the same way he'd held my daughter's while the life drained out of her. The tears I hadn't shed earlier rolled in a relentless stream down my face, soaking the neck of my T-shirt. I knew I needed to get moving, but my brain seemed disconnected from my body, thoughts whirling and diving and then floating away. I might have sat there all night, I might have sat there for the rest of my life, if someone hadn't crashed through the underbrush behind me, a slim beam of light cutting across my face. I scrambled up onto my hands and knees, feet slipping out from beneath me, and looked up to see Jenny Logan standing there. She had a shallow scratch along one cheekbone, and her breath was coming in panting gasps.

"Jesus," she said, swiping hair off her face with the hand that held a small flashlight. "It's hell getting back here."

I stared at her, had a brief moment where I wondered if I was dreaming. Was Cal even here? I looked down, saw his body at my feet, dead eyes and a ragged bullet hole in the center of his forehead. My gaze flew back to Jenny, who was looking at Cal, too.

"You did it," she said, voice even.

I croaked out something that sounded like yes.

"I'm guessing whatever reason he gave wasn't good enough." She barked out a laugh that held not even a single drop of humor. "I don't even want to know. It'll only make me angrier." She handed me the shovel clutched in her left hand. "We need to bury him," she said, matter-of-factly.

"Okay," I said, slow and slurry. I felt the shovel sliding through my numb fingers and tightened my grip on the handle. I'd been calm earlier, focused, but now I couldn't make any of the pieces fit together. "What . . . what are you doing here?"

Jenny bent down, set the flashlight on the ground. She grabbed Cal's feet and looked at me until I got the hint and laid down the shovel, grabbed his hands. "I heard you and Zach talking. When you left, I followed you. Not all the way to your mom's. You would have seen me for sure. I almost lost you when you got back on the highway and headed here. Took me a while to find where you'd parked." She was still matter-of-fact, grunting slightly as we dragged Cal's body deeper into the woods. "And then I waited until your mom showed up and dropped him off. It was a lot harder following his trail back here than I thought it would be. I got turned around a couple of times. But then I heard the gunshot. That helped. Wait a second," she said, dropped Cal's feet and ran back to grab the flashlight. She put it between her teeth and then took Cal's legs again.

We were quiet after that, other than the sound of breathing, dragging Cal through the trees.

"Here," I said, dropping his hands. "This is far enough."

Jenny took the flashlight from her mouth, peered around. "You think?"

"Yeah." I couldn't stand to touch him anymore, listen to his body scrape along the ground. And the fact was, they were either going to find him or they weren't.

Jenny went back for the shovel, and we took turns digging, the other holding the flashlight. We worked without speaking, intent on our task. When the hole was deep enough, we paused, the scent of turned earth, dark, secret things thick in the air. We dragged him to the edge and rolled him in. I flinched when he hit, but Jenny didn't. He was just the guy who'd killed her daughter. He'd never been the one who held that same daughter and rocked her to sleep, or gave her a bath and blew bubbles until she squealed. Jenny had never loved him.

Filling in the grave should have gone faster, been easier, but it seemed to progress in slow motion, both of us exhausted and ready to be done. When Jenny had scooped the final bit of earth, we spread moss and twigs over the site, walked and kicked until it looked the same as the rest of the ground. Or at least same enough.

Jenny palmed dirt off her cheek with the back of her hand. "That's it." She looked at me. "Anything you want to say?" She gestured toward the grave with a dirt-stained hand.

What was there to say? He'd been my brother. My first love. The only person I'd ever trusted not to hurt me. "Yeah," I said, grabbing the shovel off the ground. "He had it coming."

I had to hand it to my mama, those words I'd sworn I'd never say were strangely satisfying on my tongue.

. . .

Jenny had done a good job hiding her car, although the chances of anyone happening along here were slim. I put the shovel in her trunk, and she tossed the flashlight in as well. "I'll wash the shovel as soon as I get home," she said. "Put it right back in the garage." She glanced down at her dirt-streaked clothes with a wince. "And get rid of these."

I looked at her. "Are you going to hold it together? Once daylight hits and all this is real?"

She stared back at me. "It's already real. And yeah, I'll hold it together fine."

"What about Zach?" I asked. "He knew it was Cal."

Jenny leaned back against her car. I could barely make out her features in the moonlight. "Don't worry about Zach. The second I came out of the kitchen and told him I'd heard you two, the only thing he could focus on was the fact that now I knew he was Junie's father. 'What she said was true about that night, it was only one time. You and I weren't even engaged yet. It never happened again.'" She snorted out a laugh. "Like I give a shit about that, at this point. It was years ago. They're gone. Who cares? But Zach is Zach. He'll carry his guilt around like a hair shirt for the foreseeable future." She turned and opened the driver's door. "I can use that, if I have to. But I don't think I will."

"For what it's worth, he never really wanted to keep Junie a secret from you. That was my idea. I didn't see what good it would do for anyone to know."

Jenny gave me a little smile. "They found each other anyway, didn't they? Zach and Junie. Junie and Izzy. Looking back, I feel like an idiot for not seeing it. The way he was always hovering around them when Junie was at our house, hanging on every word she said. I finally know why he never wanted to leave Barren Springs. It was written all over his face."

"What was?" I asked.

"Love," Jenny said. "He loved her."

It should have eased something in me, the knowledge that Junie'd had a father who loved her after all. Junie, who'd never once voiced a complaint about being fatherless, but whose eyes always followed men carrying babies, men with kids balanced on their shoulders. But all I felt was sorrow. My heart ached for my daughter, for Zach, for all of us. For the secrets we'd kept from each other, for the chances we'd never had. I'd thought I was doing the right thing for Junie all those years ago, but maybe I had robbed her without meaning to.

"What will you tell Zach about tonight?" I asked. "We need to have our stories straight."

"That we went to talk to Cal, but we couldn't find him. Spent half the night tracking him down, but came up empty. I'll tell him that during that time we hashed it out and we're not even sure anymore he had anything to do with it."

"And he'll believe that?"

Jenny slid into her seat and put her key in the ignition. "Sure he will. Because he'll want to. Because he'll need to. He wasn't lying earlier. He's not equipped for this kind of thing. But he needs to believe we aren't, either."

"I didn't think you were," I told her. Which wasn't entirely true. I remembered her expression when she'd spoken about Matt and Izzy in her kitchen. The death wish written on her face. And I knew this place, this patch of land. It didn't breed many weaklings. She might have grown up in an actual house and never seriously wondered where her next meal was coming from, but here you got strong fast or you didn't make it.

Jenny smiled, white teeth in a dirt-streaked face, all bite and no joy. "I'm capable of anything, I guess. When someone pushes me far enough." She tapped her steering wheel with both hands. "You and your mama can handle Land?"

"Yeah, Mama has his number start to finish. I think she's the only person he's scared of, other than maybe Jimmy Ray. But she's gonna leave Cal's car at her place, let it sit there. If Land comes sniffing around, she'll tell him Cal showed up today, all antsy, told her he had somewhere to be, and then some guy in a dark gray truck came and picked him up. Last she's seen or heard from him."

"That'll probably be good enough for Land. His lazy ass isn't going to waste time looking for Cal, especially if you and your mama aren't squawking about him being gone."

"I thought you liked Land," I said, surprised.

"No one likes Land," Jenny said. "But we needed him, or thought we did, so I played nice. It about killed me, though. I've hated him since I was a teenager. When I was sixteen, he caught me sneaking out of my house. Told me if I gave him a blow job he wouldn't tell my parents."

"What did you do?" My voice sounded far away.

"I threatened to tell his wife, but that didn't seem to faze him. Now that I think about it, she'd probably have thanked me for saving her from having to do the dirty work. So I told him to go fuck himself. I figured a grounding from my dad was better than putting my mouth anywhere near Land. I had another choice and I took it. But I doubt everyone he runs into has the same luck."

I paused, wondering how much, if anything, to tell her. Decided that after tonight Land was hardly a secret worth keeping anymore. "I definitely didn't."

Jenny's eyes flew to mine. "When?" she asked.

I made a noncommittal noise. "Years ago."

"Well, something tells me if there's a next time, it'll be a different story."

I nodded, and she reached out, laid her hand on my arm. "We did the right thing, Eve. We did good by our girls. It doesn't bring them back." She took a deep breath, released it. "But it helps, somehow."

When she drove away, I stood on the weedy verge and watched her taillights fade, knowing somehow that my story wouldn't intersect with hers again. But I'd always look at her differently now, when I heard her name around town or caught a flash of dark hair in the distance. I had a feeling that before long Zach and Jenny would disappear from Barren Springs, finally venture out into the wider world. But wherever they ended up, she and I would remain interwoven. Not by our daughters' deaths. And not by their shared father. But by this night—the dark and the earth and a man's body between us. By our unflinching ability to do what was necessary.

TWENTY-FIVE

My mama was waiting for me on her trailer steps, her cigarette a glowing beacon in the dark. I sank down next to her, dirt clinging to the webs of my fingers, shoved deep under my nails. My back and shoulders ached something fierce, and I knew there'd be hell to pay tomorrow, in every kind of way. I already couldn't picture a world without my brother in it.

"Girl, you are a mess," my mama said. "Don't smell too good, neither. You can shower before you go. Leave those clothes here and borrow something of mine." She held out her hand, and I passed her the gun. We'd already decided that it was safer for her to get rid of it. That way, if I was arrested, I wouldn't be tempted to spill my guts about where the gun ended up. And we wanted it someplace far away from where Cal's body was buried, just in case. These woods were vast, filled with caves and caverns, and I trusted Mama to find a good spot for it. One that would take decades, maybe lifetimes, for anyone to uncover. "Money's inside," she told me. "Don't forget to take it."

We'd already decided that part, too. How tomorrow morning I was gonna go into Land's office with the money and tell him I'd found it at Cal's. I hadn't been snooping, swear to God. I'd been cleaning out his closet, trying to keep myself occupied, and the vacuum caught on the edge of the carpet and there it was. I was freaked out, took the money without thinking, left the carpet and the mess and got out of there. I'd tried to ask Cal about it, but couldn't find him. And when I went back to his place later, it was cleared out. His clothes gone. He must have come home, seen the money was missing, and panicked. I wasn't sure what was going on, what to do about the money, but figured Land would help.

"Help himself to the money, more like," my mama had muttered when we'd devised this part of the plan. But we couldn't see a good way around it. The money was the way to keep Land quiet. A little windfall and no talk-of-the-town embarrassment about how his deputy had been putting one over on him all this time. Of course, I had no doubt Mama had lightened the stash while I was gone. But I didn't want any part of it. Every dollar stained with Junie's blood.

Even knowing my mama, I expected her to say something. To ask about Cal's last moments or express some kind of pain. But she didn't. She finished her beer and then led me inside for a shower. When I was cleaned up, dressed in a pair of her jeans and one of her faded T-shirts, I took the bag of money and paused at the screen door. The air was warmer than it had been only a week ago, summer barreling toward us fast as a runaway train. Sweat and stagnant air and legs pockmarked with mosquito bites just over the horizon.

In a blink, autumn, leaves turning gold and amber, scent of wood smoke in the air. And then winter, ice on the roads and bitter chill sneaking under my door at night. The seasons would keep on passing, the days and weeks and months rolling on, taking me further and further from my daughter. Until one day, sooner than I could comprehend, I would have lived with her absence longer than her presence. Her life a brief, shining light fading into shadow.

My mama stopped me at the door, laid a cold hand on my cheek. Her eyes were clear, glowing. She was proud of me, I realized with a start. Maybe for the first and only time in my life. For doing a hard thing well. For doing an awful thing easily.

"You my daughter again?" she asked, voice raspy.

"Yeah, Mama," I said, because it was the truth. And because sometimes you had to pick your poison. Weigh all the available options and choose the one that killed you least. Take a long, honest look at yourself and own the darkness that lived inside. "I'm your daughter. Always."

I opened the door and stepped out into the night.

THE BEGINNING

Somehow, she hadn't thought her daughter would be this small. She'd seen baby girls all her life, boys, too. Women birthed them like puppies around here. First one barely walking before the next one came along. But when they belonged to other people, they seemed sturdier, less fragile. This one in her arms, her daughter, looked delicate as glass.

The baby snuffled a little, burrowing against her chest, seeking. She had a sudden urge to pinch her daughter, show her, right from the start, that the world was full of ugly things. That way her daughter wouldn't be surprised later, wouldn't be weak, expecting the world to do her any favors. Trying, in the best way she knew how, to teach her daughter something worth learning.

"Sorry, little girl," she whispered against the baby's downy cheek. She'd forgotten how sweet newborn babies smelled. "You're stuck with me." She'd seen the mothers who coddled, who passed out hugs and kisses like confetti. And that was never going to be her. Didn't see what good it did, fawning over kids that way, making them think they were special, that life wouldn't kick their asses the same as everyone else. She didn't know how to coddle, but she knew how to forge. How to make her daughter strong. She couldn't give her much, but she could give her that. Because, pinch or no pinch, the world *was* ugly, especially for girls. There was no escaping it. You either fought back or you surrendered. And no daughter of hers was going to surrender. No daughter of hers was going to lie down and take it. Not if she had anything to say about it.

The midwife from up the road, who'd taken payment in booze and a crumpled twenty, wandered in, hands still streaked with blood. "You settled on a name yet?"

She looked down at her daughter. "Eve," she said. "Her name is Eve."

ACKNOWLEDGMENTS

First and foremost, a huge thank-you to my family: Brian, Graham, and Quinn. This book could not have been written without your love, support, and encouragement. The three of you make my life better every single day. Thank you also to my mom, Mary Anne; my in-laws, Fran and Larry; and all my extended family. My father didn't live long enough to see this book in print, but he asked me how the writing was coming every time we talked. I still feel him cheering me on whenever I sit down at my computer. Thank you to Holly, my best friend and most trusted confidante. You somehow manage endless patience with me whenever I'm in the throes of writing a new book. I am so thankful for you and our friendship. And to my SPs, Meshelle, Michelle, and Trish, thank you for always listening, making fun of me when I need a laugh, and bottomless margaritas when I need a break. Thanks also to Laura McHugh, who understands the writing life and the frustrations and joys that come along with it. Your e-mails helped me more than you know.

Jodi, thank you for your wisdom, wit, and willingness to tell me to stop overthinking and start writing. I feel very lucky to have an agent I also consider a dear friend. To my editor, Maya Ziv, this is our first book together, but I sincerely hope it's only the first of many. You have been a delight to work with. Smart, funny, and passionate about what you do. Thank you for making this process such fun. And heartfelt thanks to Christine Ball, John Parsley, Leigh Butler, Sabila Kahn, Hannah Feeney, Emily Canders, Elina Vaysbeyn, and everyone at Dutton and Penguin Random House. I am forever grateful for your enthusiasm, professionalism, and your support of me and my books.

To all the readers, librarians, booksellers, and bloggers, thank you for reading, reviewing, recommending, and getting the word out. None of us would be here without you.

And, as always, thank you to Larry the cat, who still keeps my legs warm while I'm writing.

ABOUT THE AUTHOR

Amy Engel is the author of *The Roanoke Girls* and The Book of Ivy series. A former criminal defense attorney, she lives outside of Kansas City, Missouri, with her husband and children.